# DARK
# MEN

# DARK
# MEN

DEREK HAAS

PEGASUS CRIME
NEW YORK

DARK MEN

Pegasus Crime is an Imprint of
Pegasus Books Ltd
148 West 37th Street, 13th Floor
New York, NY 10018

Copyright © 2011 Derek Haas

First Pegasus Books cloth edition December 2011

Interior design by Maria Fernandez

Library of Congress Cataloging-in-Publication Data is available.

ISBN: 978-1-60598-390-5

10 9 8 7 6 5 4 3 2 1

Printed in the United States of America
Distributed by W. W. Norton & Company

*For Bruno, who premiered.*
*And for Augie, the sequel.*

# DARK
# MEN

## CHAPTER ONE

**W**ould you listen to a story told by a dying man? Would you listen to me tell it in the present, like it is happening now? It seems I've been telling my story and living my story for so long, the two have mixed, and I'm no longer sure which is accurate, which informs the other: the story or the life. I try to tell it the way it happened, as it is happening, but how close am I to the truth?

I'll do my best to finish, to give you closure. You've been with me this long; I owe you that. But at some point, forgive me if my story suddenly ends.

In Fresno, California, in 2007, a tiger mauled a woman. The tiger was six years old and had arrived in the United States as a pet purchased by Lori Nagel through dubious channels in the Far East. Her friends told investigators the tiger was quite docile toward Lori, even affectionate, right up to the moment its five-inch dew claw severed an artery in Lori's left leg. She survived, but her leg didn't. She insisted the unfortunate incident was her fault; it was her carelessness, her inattentiveness that was the cause. Nevertheless, at the behest of animal control, a veterinarian euthanized the beast a few weeks after the incident.

The tiger's only crime was being a goddamn tiger.

A little over two years has passed since Risina Lorenzana and I moved to the little village on the sea. I am still here. It is the longest I have lived in one place, and I have almost stopped looking over my shoulder. Instincts die hard, however, and for most of my life, I've survived by keeping my guard up, my defenses engaged. I spent my youth incarcerated in a juvenile detention center named Waxham outside of Boston, Massachusetts; my adult life I spent as a contract killer, and a damned good one at that. I was what the Russians call a Silver Bear, a hit man who never defaults on a job, who takes any assignment no matter how difficult, and who commands top fees for his work. As such, I survived this professional life by honing my peripheral vision. I killed, I escaped, and when hunters came for me, I put them down.

Risina changed everything. She gave me a glimpse of what my life could be without a Glock in my hand, and when the opportunity arose to break free, I leapt at it.

She's the only one who knows my complete story, the only one alive who knows my true name.

I crack an egg, and the yolk spills out whole into a white bowl. A little salt, a little milk, a quick stir with a fork, and I pour the contents on to a pan set on low heat. Risina walks out of the bedroom, yawning, tying her black hair up so I can see all of her neck. When she puts her hands up, her pajama top pulls away from the bottoms, exposing her stomach, and something in me stirs. It's been over two years, and something in me always stirs.

"You've finally given up on my cooking." Her Italian accent has softened, but only a bit, like the hint of spice in a pot of strong coffee. She pours herself some juice and plops down in a mismatched sofa chair we bought off a yard in a neighboring town.

"I'm just giving you a breather."

"Ha. You can tell me the truth."

"I'd rather not."

She laughs. "I'm terrible, I know. But I'm getting better."

Risina has forged a relationship with a fisherman's wife, Kaimi, one of the few village natives to venture to our house after we settled. Kaimi's a plump woman, with a broad forehead and a broad smile. She's been teaching Risina the basics of cooking—how to season the meat before grilling it, how to add spices to the pot before boiling the water—but it's a bit like teaching music to a deaf man. Risina can get the mechanics right, but for some reason, the end result is as flavorless as cardboard.

Still, she continues to try, undaunted. Her inability to get frustrated fascinates me. Maybe it's an indigenous side effect to this place, where the rhythm of the day is always a few beats slower, a few notes softer. Or maybe it's just Risina, whose beauty has grown even more pronounced since we arrived. Something unnamed has relaxed inside her, and her inner calm now wafts off her in waves. She always had an underlying sadness just below the surface on her face, in her eyes, but it seems to have diminished like her accent. The sun has brought out the gold in her skin, and the simple dresses and the longer way she wears her hair combine to make her look even more radiant and alive.

I look decent. I've kept in shape by running on the beach and swimming in the water. My body's not as hard as it was, but I'm far from sluggish.

Kaimi's husband Ariki heads to his boat six days a week. He leaves his home before the sun rises, and walks into the town center before descending the cobblestone path to the bamboo huts that dot the dock. Here he cuts bait until 5:45, and then he pilots his long boat out to deeper water, alone, waiting for the sun to arrive and the fish to start biting.

I followed him from the shadows for five days once. I tracked him carefully, noting points that held the highest probability of success. I could kill him shortly after he leaves his house, drag his body to the jungle and have him buried before anyone else awakens. I could lie in wait at one of his favorite fishing spots, have him come to me, then shoot him and weigh his body down so it never floats to the surface. I could wait until Kaimi leaves to do her laundry and waylay him in his own shower after a long day on the water, when the man is at his most vulnerable.

I have no intention of killing Ariki, ever. But I'm keeping in shape in other ways, too.

Once every three months, I head to the only city of any size on this side of the country. I amass several things we're lacking: clothes, batteries, light bulbs and other assorted knick-knacks. But the true purpose of these trips is to stock up on the one necessity Risina can't do without: books. She's given up so much of her life to escape with me. Literature is like a lifeline for her, a connection with everything she left behind. When I met her, she was acquiring rare books for a small shop named Zodelli on the Via Poli in Rome, and the job was more than an occupation to her; it was a passion, a necessity, a fix. Something I understand well. Her dark eyes dance whenever I return with a few dozen hard covers, half written in her native Italian, half written in English. She makes a list of ten authors she wants me to find before I set out—Goethe and Poe and Dickens and Twain and Moravia—and leaves the rest of the purchases to my discretion. It takes me hours to make my selections, ranging from contemporary authors like Wolfe and Mailer and King, to my favorite writer, Steinbeck. I get no greater pleasure than opening the boxes for Risina when I return and then watch the color rise in her cheeks. In minutes, she is curled in a chair, her feet tucked under her, absorbed in the fresh pages.

I am near the front of the bookstore, a half-dozen classics in my hand, when I first notice a man marking me. He's a black guy with a wide face and a freshly purchased linen shirt. I can still make out the starched fold lines, since the shirt hasn't been washed.

The city attracts its share of tourists, but this man is no vacationer. I can see it in his hard eyes and the stiff way he holds his shoulders. He's watching me, only me, in the glass across the street, I'm sure of it. If he's trying to be stealthy, he's not very practiced at it.

My heartbeat slowly rises, and I have to admit, it's a welcome feeling, like finding an old jacket in the closet and discovering it still fits. Fuck, this is not right . . . I should be angry, worried, embarrassed I've been discovered, that my hard-fought-for independence has suddenly been compromised without warning. So why am I feeling the complete opposite? Why do I feel elated?

Over a year ago, Risina and I lit out for a remote sanctuary following an assignment in which I killed an innocent bystander along with my target. The unfortunate man had a brother who hired a host of assassins to track me down—to hunt the hunter—and when I killed the brother too and disposed of the final assassin, I thought I was free. I fled that world, persuading the girl I loved to escape with me.

But did I convince myself? Did I really want to escape?

The tiger is still a tiger.

I move out of the cashier's line and head back over to the classics shelf in the rear of the store to see if my movements elicit a response.

Like I thought, he's an amateur; he jerks his head to track my position, as conspicuous as if he'd rung a bell. I pull out my cell phone, pretend to check who is phoning me, then put the phone to my ear and pantomime a conversation while I really snap photos of the man through the window. They may not be perfect shots, but they should be enough.

A clerk stands near the back, sorting new arrivals.

"Bathroom?" I ask in her language and she points me to a short hallway. I quickly pass it and duck out the delivery entrance, slipping into an alley. I hurry to the nearest intersection where the alley meets the driveway and wait.

I don't have a weapon, so I'm going to have to use his.

I hear his hurried footsteps approaching, and I am right, he's an amateur, no doubt about that. If he's been in this line of work, he hasn't been doing it long. He's making as much noise as a fireworks display. In another minute, he won't be making any noise at all.

He swings around the corner in a dead sprint, and it only takes a solid kick to his trailing leg to send him sprawling, limbs akimbo, like a skier tumbling down a mountain. Before he can right himself, I am on him, pinning him to the cement with my knee in the small of his back. A quick sweep of his waist and I have his gun, a cheap chrome pistol I'm sure he bought in the last day or two, after arriving in the country. A second later, it is out and up and pointed at the back of his head.

Before I can pull the trigger, he shouts "Columbus!"

I roll him over and have the gun under his chin. His eyes in that wide face are wild, feral, like a cornered wolf. No, whatever he is, he's no professional.

"What do you want?" I spit through clenched teeth. I like him scared and I mean to keep him that way.

"I came to find you . . ."

"No shit," and I thumb the hammer back, cocking the pistol. I hope the gun isn't so cheap as to spring before I'm ready to pull the trigger. I want to find out who the hell this guy is who knows my name and how on earth he found me before I plant him.

He winces, his face screwing up like he tasted a lemon, and then he bellows, "For Archie. For Archibald Grant . . . your old fence!"

Whatever I was expecting, it wasn't that.

"Archie?"

"Yeah man, that's what I'm trying to tell you. Archie's been taken."

We sit in the back of a chicken-and-pork restaurant, drinking San Miguels.

"What's your name?"

"I go by Smoke."

And as if the mention of his name turns his thoughts, he pulls out a pack of Fortunes, pops free a cigarette, and lights it with a shaky hand. I guess he hasn't quite calmed his nerves after having his own gun cocked beneath his chin.

"Then tell me something straight, Smoke . . . you're no bagman."

He blows a thin stream out of the side of his mouth. "No . . . shit no. I just handled things for Archie . . . a 'my-man-Friday' type setup. Whatever he needed me to track down, that was my job."

"A fence in training."

He nods. "I thought about trying my hand at the killing business, but I wasn't sure I had the chops for it."

"Now you know."

"You're right about that."

"How'd you find me?"

"Archie liked to tell stories about you, said you were the best he'd ever seen. Said if he ever got in a tight spot, I's to open an envelope he kept in a safety deposit box at Harris Bank on Wabash. That'd tell me where to find you. He told me this pretty soon after I started there . . ."

"How long . . . ?"

"Over a year. After his sister died, he came back to Chicago a bit lost. I knew him from his prison days."

Ruby. His sister's name was Ruby, and she was one of the good ones. I had a real fondness for her; I like to think we were cut from the same cloth. Then Ruby had caught a bullet in that mess in Italy two years ago that made me want to leave the game forever. And here it was, all coming back.

"I meant, how long has Archie been missing?"

"Not missing. Taken. There's a note."

He shifts to reach into his pants pocket and withdraws a single sheet of paper, folded into quarters, then hands it over without the slightest hesitation. As I unfold it, he takes another drag, squinting his left eye as the smoke blows past it, toward the ceiling.

"Goddamn, it's nice to smoke indoors. They don't let us do that shit in Chicago no more."

The sheet is standard white typing paper, the kind found jamming copy machines throughout the world. Block letters, written in a masculine hand with a black Sharpie:

BRING COLUMBUS HOME. OR YOU'LL GET GRANT BACK IN A WAY YOU WON'T LIKE.

I look up, and Smoke is studying my face.

"Why didn't you tell me this was about me?"

Smoke shrugs. "I'm telling you now."

When I level my eyes, he puts his palms up like a victim in a robbery. "I didn't mean nothing by it. Just didn't know how you'd react. They ask for you and I immediately come find you. I wasn't looking to do an investigation . . . wouldn't know where to begin. But your name was on there clear as crystal and this seemed like a straight-up emergency, so here I am. Didn't want you to have the wrong idea."

"When was the last time you saw Archie?"

"I was at his place the night before . . . wasn't unusual for us to be up 'til eleven-thirty, twelve, goin' over all the goin's on, but mostly talking shit, you know? I think I left around midnight, but I don't remember looking at a clock. It was late, though.

"Next day I was supposed to meet him for eggs and bacon at Sam & George's on North Lincoln, but Archie never showed."

"That unusual?"

"First time ever. I knew something was up before the waitress set down the menus. He always beat me there. Always. Say what you want about Archibald Grant, but he's a punctual son-of-a-cuss."

I couldn't argue with that. "So what'd you do?"

"I got up, left a buck on the table for coffee, and headed to Archie's place. Banged on the door, but no answer. The lock wasn't forced or nothing, so I opened it and poked my head in."

"You have a key?"

"Yeah. Archie gave me one." He says it defensively, but I shake him off like a pitcher shaking off a sign from the plate.

"Keep going."

"Not a sound in the joint. Air as still as a morgue."

"No sign of a struggle?"

"Not in the front room, no." He leans forward, lowers his voice. "But in the bedroom, he must've put up a hell of a fight. Blood everywhere, lamps knocked over, mirror broke, bed knocked to shit. I knew it was bad, bad, bad. My first thought was he was dead, truth be told. All that blood. Someone must've stuck him and dragged the body away. But then I saw the note."

"Where?"

"Living room table." He tamps out another cigarette from his pack and lights it off the end of the first, dropping the original into a plastic ashtray when he's done.

"You think the note was put there for you to find it?"

"Don't know who else it'd be for. I'm the only one he lets into his house."

"And you have absolutely no idea who did this or why they want me?"

"Swear on every single family member's name, living and dead."

As a professional killer, I have to read faces the way a surgeon examines x-rays. A purse of the lips, a downward glance of the eyes, a nervous tap of the knee, there are dozens of tells that give away when a man is playing fast and loose with the truth. Smoke is skittish, no mistake, but his voice is steady and his eyes are focused. He's afraid of me, but he's telling the truth.

The air is dry and stale and the cigarette smoke hangs under the ceiling like a gas cloud, thick and poisoned.

I tap the note with my index finger. "And you have no idea why they want me?"

"I hung around that place for two days, hoping someone would show up and explain things further, but not a creature was stirring, you know what I'm saying? On the third day, I went looking in that safety deposit box."

"No one followed you to the bank?"

A look sweeps over his face like the thought never crossed his mind. His adam's apple dips like a yo-yo.

"No. I mean . . . no . . . I don't think so." Like he's trying to convince himself.

"Doesn't matter," I say so he'll get back on track.

"Anyway, that's where I found the file on you."

"What's your plan from here?"

Smoke shrugs as he starts on his third cigarette. "Man, I wish I knew. Like I said, Archie told me if he's ever in a tight spot, to set out to find you. And then your name's on this here note. I don't know what to tell you, but you gotta admit, this qualifies as a pretty goddamned tight spot, so I did what Archie asked. Beyond that . . ."

He lets his voice spool out, joining the smoke near the ceiling like he never intended to finish the sentence.

An image pops into my head, a highway in Nevada I drove a lifetime ago. The sky was clear, the desert calm, and the blacktop was an infinite line across the landscape, a shapeless, endless mirage. Each time I'd crest a bit of a slope or round a slight bend, the line would reemerge before me, stretching out to the horizon, teasing me, sentient, like it knew I could never reach its end.

I am about to drive that road again. I knew it the moment Smoke called me by name. The real question, the one I'm not sure I want to answer: did I ever truly leave it in the first place?

Risina is folding clothes in the back room when I enter, and her face lights up when she sees me coming through the door.

"What'd you bring me?"

Then she spots it in my face, and I guess she's believed this day would come since we first arrived.

"Someone found you."

I nod.

"How much time do we have?"

I swallow, my mouth chalky. "We leave tonight."

"Where?"

"I have to go to the U.S. for a while."

"What's a while?"

"I don't know."

"And me?"

"I don't know."

She folds her arms across her chest and raises her chin. She's never been one to lower her eyes, and she's not going to start now. "Tell me what happened."

I paint the picture of Smoke, about the way he found me and what he had to say about Archibald Grant and the note left behind that called me out by name.

"You told me you were out . . . that Archie wanted you out, was covering for you, he said. I don't understand this. His problems are not your problems."

"I was out. I am. But he stitched me up when I needed stitching and I can't turn my back on him."

Risina collapses into a chair, but still she doesn't lower her eyes.

"I want you to know . . ." I start but she cuts me off.

"Give me a moment to think, dammit." This might be the first time she's ever snapped at me, and I can't say I blame her. "Can you bring me some water?"

I move to the kitchen and pour some filtered water out of a jug we keep in the refrigerator. This might be the last time I'm in this kitchen, the last time I open this fridge, and even though this place isn't much, it has been good to us. Better not to think this way. This is no time for sentiment. Better to rip the bandage off quickly.

I return with the water. She takes it absently and drinks the entire glass without taking it from her lips. I'm not sure she even knows I'm in the room. I can see her eyes darting as her mind catches up to what I told her.

After a moment, she finally raises her eyes and focuses on me, maybe to keep the room from spinning. She blushes, blood rising in her cheeks.

"I'm sorry . . . this is new to me. I thought I was prepared, had prepared myself for something like this, but . . ."

She swallows and bites her lip. I know she is sorting her thoughts the way a contract bridge player organizes playing cards, bringing all the suits together before laying down the next play.

"Are you going to have to kill someone?"

"I don't know."

"What if once you enter this life, you don't want to stop again?"

She's trying to read my face, less interested in what I say than how I look when I say it. It's a skill she's picked up from me. I answer with the truth.

"I don't know."

She absorbs this like a physical blow. Just when I don't think she's going to say anything, she finds her voice. There is a strength there that shouldn't surprise me, though it does.

"I'm coming with you."

"I don't—"

"It's not a question. I'm not asking for permission. I'm coming with you. You offered me a life with you and I won't run away just because the past caught up with us. *Us*. Not you. Us."

"Risina—"

"You can't send me away. You can't kick me in the stomach like you did the first girl you loved." Her eyes are hot now. "I'm coming."

I turn my voice to gravel. She hasn't heard this voice from me, but I want the weight behind my words to be clear. "It's one thing to hear these stories about me and another to live them, to see them with your own eyes. I can't get back into this and have to worry about—"

She interrupts, fearlessly, her voice matching mine. If I thought I could outgravel her, I misjudged the woman I love. "Yes, you will. You'll learn to do it *and* worry about me at the same time. I'm not giving you the choice."

"You'll see a side of me you won't recognize."

"Don't you understand a damn thing I'm saying? I want to know *every* side of you. I must know! I've wanted *all* of you since I first met you. Not just one side or the other. Not just the mask you choose to show me."

"And what if you hate what you see?"

"I won't."

"And what if you die standing next to me?"

"Then I'll die. People do it every day."

I start to ask another question and stop myself. There's a reason I fell in love with Risina the first time I saw her; it's here before me now. Defiance, ambition, determination, passion . . . the qualities of confidence. The qualities of a professional assassin. A tiger is a goddamned tiger. The beasts are born that way, and no matter how they are *nurtured*, their *nature* always emerges eventually.

"So when do we leave?" she asks.

"Now," I whisper.

# CHAPTER TWO

It takes us a few days to buy passports. Although Smoke failed spectacularly as a bagman, he's not a bad fence. He's been with Archie Grant long enough to know how to scrounge the right information, ask the right questions, navigate the world beneath the world, the one where money exchanges hands and lips stay tight.

This is all new to Risina, and she adjusts, acting normally, with just a hint of boredom, the way she must've negotiated competitively for a rare book. An Italian fence named Vespucci once told me, "no matter the situation, act like you've been there before." Risina says little and keeps her face emotionless, neutral. Even as we're engaged in something as simple as obtaining illegal papers, she looks like she's done it a thousand times. Maybe she's a natural. I won't deny that I feel, well, proud of her. Maybe that's irrational, but I don't care.

In a hotel near the airport, we lie in bed, waiting on a morning flight.

"I don't want you to get too confident. We haven't done anything yet."

"How do you want me to be?"

"Observant."

She widens her eyes. "Like this?" She holds it for a moment before breaking into a smile.

"I'm serious."

"Yes, babe. I know. You're going to be tense and I understand that. This is the new man. The one who has to worry about someone besides himself. But when we're alone, then I'm going to want *you* back. Not Columbus."

She pulls close to me and buries her nose in my neck.

"I wasn't aware this was a democracy."

"Well, now you are."

"As long as you understand that when we leave this room, or any room, I'm in charge. You look to me. You learn from me."

"I understand."

"I mean it, Risina."

"I know you do. And I answered you that I understand."

She sleeps peacefully, as though this is just another night in the fishing village. Maybe she's going to be okay in this world. Maybe she'll learn quickly and take direction and thrive. Maybe if I keep telling myself that over and over, I'll believe it.

Chicago is warm but stale, like a mausoleum releasing hundreds of years of trapped air after the front stone is rolled away. It must be the exhaust from the traffic in the city or the wind off the lake, or maybe the smell is just in my head. My temples throb like someone is tapping my head with a hammer.

Risina sits next to me in the rental sedan—a dark blue economy car—staring out the window, smiling absently.

I let her come. She insisted, but the decision was, is, mine. I could have blown off Smoke, protested I was out, truly out, that Archie's problems were Archie's problems, taken Risina and fled to another isolated country, but the truth is . . . I didn't want to. I'm like Eve staring at the picked apple, but that's not quite the right metaphor. I've already tasted the apple and instead of facing banishment, I've been offered passage back into Eden, or into my definition of paradise anyway. But at what price? There is always a price.

"I'm going to say something and I don't want you to protest or argue or answer. Just nod your head that you agree when I finish."

She waits, and I can feel her eyes.

"This is my decision to have you with me. To teach you what I do. To bring you into this world. Okay? I take responsibility for it. I own it."

She waits until I turn my head her way before she nods. Whether or not she agrees with me, I think I see understanding in her eyes. Regardless, I had to say it.

I've never had a charge before, and I want it defined and out in the open, as much for me as for her. I have to teach her, protect her, and lead her all at once, and I will not take these obligations lightly.

Straight from the airport, Smoke leads us to Archie's apartment. I check the side-view mirrors, looking for patterns in the traffic behind us, but I don't think anyone knows about our arrival. If the plan of the kidnappers was to tail Smoke and strike as soon as he found me, then they've done a lousy job. There's no tail from what I can see, and I didn't clock anyone back at the bookstore or restaurant before we left our hiding spot.

I've been inside Archie's building a couple of times before, once after killing a couple of his rival fences, and another time after I was shot in the ribs in a Chicago Public Library. Grant hired a private surgeon to stitch me up, and his sister Ruby took care of me until I got back on my feet. That was years ago, before I quit and before Ruby took a bullet to the face and died in front of a church in Siena as I stood next to her.

The apartment is as I remember it and as Smoke described. There's dried blood in the bedroom, the color of rust, and several pieces of furniture—a lamp, a nightstand—are overturned.

"I didn't touch nothing," Smoke says. "This is just as I found it."

I scan the room, then zero in on a chest of drawers and put my finger in a smooth hole.

"Shit. Is that a bullet hole? I didn't *even* see that." He hits the word "even" to make sure I hear the truth in his voice.

"Can you help me move this?"

The back of the chest and the wall behind it have the same hole. Risina watches, fascinated.

"You got a little knife on you?" I say to Smoke.

He immediately shakes his head, but then thinks. "Hold on a second . . ."

He scampers back to the kitchen and Risina smiles and nods, rocking forward on her toes. "I'm impressed."

"In this job, you have to look at a scene of violence, the aftermath, and read it like a book. I want you to try to visualize what happened in this room. On your own, no help from me."

I hear Smoke rummaging around in kitchen drawers, but I focus on Risina. Her eyes trace the room, drinking it in, and I can see her gears turning.

"I don't know. There was a fight, and someone was shot."

"Not shot. I don't think so. We'd see a different blood pattern on the floor, on the walls. When someone takes a bullet, a part of his insides usually comes out. So you'd see some other matter besides blood."

"Then what do you think? He was stabbed?"

Before I can answer, Smoke returns holding a small kitchen knife, a screwdriver, and a letter opener, presenting all three items like a kid excited to please his teacher.

"The opener," I say. A few minutes later and I fish the bullet out of the wall, then toss it to Risina. "That's a .22 slug. Look at the size of it and try to commit it to memory. It's a low caliber round out of a small gun. An assassin's weapon. I'll get ahold of some other calibers so you can compare them."

I turn to Smoke. "Archie have a .22?"

"Yeah."

"He keep it under the mattress?"

"Yeah."

I lift it up, but the gun isn't there.

"Well, he got one shot off before they fought over the pistol. I'm saying 'they' 'cause I'm guessing it was at least two guys."

"Why?"

"Well, I could be wrong, but I think one held him up while the other one went to work on his face. That's why you have the blood here, in a circle, after they broke his nose and most likely knocked him out. They held him up while his head hung. It's hard to hold an unconscious guy still, and his head lolled a bit. That accounts for why there is so much blood on the floor. A stab wound would pour straight down and soak the victim's clothes. A broken nose? That's a gusher, and if they're holding him upright, it's just going to get everywhere."

It's Smoke's turn to ask a question. "Why would they do that?"

I shrug. "They wanted information on me and the muscle went too far? They wanted to beat on him for putting up a fight, pulling a gun? Who knows? But they were careful not to step in the blood, which means the fist work happened after the initial fight. Anyway, none of this matters all that much until we figure out who's holding Archie and why they want me."

Risina turns the bullet over in her fingers and holds it up close to her eye like a jeweler examining a diamond. "But we know now it was more than one guy."

"We know it was more than one guy here in the room. But maybe they were only hired muscle . . . not necessarily the guy looking for me. Either way, the person who wanted Archie snuck two or more guys into this place, which is no easy feat, I know from experience, and got them out of the building while transporting an unconscious resident."

"They're professionals. Like you."

I nod and chew my lip. I had come to that conclusion within five seconds of entering the room, but I wanted Risina to arrive at it on her own.

"So what now?"

"Now we bang on a door."

Bo Willis is a big man, not quite forty, who looks like his monthly trip to the pharmacy includes a permanent prescription for Lipitor. He was a Chicago cop for twelve years but quit when he didn't make detective the second year in a row. Being a cop means taking a lot of ribbing from your fellow officers, and I'm sure he received his fair share after failing his detective exams or getting passed over. Bo joined a private security firm, the kind that requires short-sleeve blue uniforms and patches with names on them. He was content to punch the clock and collect his sixty-five a year, though he did it with a scowl on his face. His first couple of years he spent on a bench at an airport warehouse. The last three, he held down an Aero chair behind a security console in Archibald Grant's building.

We didn't have to knock on his door; Bo eats breakfast each morning at a place called Willard's Diner, occupying a booth near the front where he can spread out his newspaper. He looks up for a moment when Risina walks by, and follows her with his eyes until she passes. I want her to hear my conversation with the security guard, but I make a mental note that I'm going to have to talk to her about her appearance. In a business where invisibility is a weapon, I can't afford to have Risina turning heads by simply walking into the room.

I give Bo a few minutes to settle into the sports page and then slide into the booth opposite him. He starts, unused to having his territory invaded, and that's a good place to put him: uncomfortable, on defense before he even knows he's entered the arena.

"This is my booth, guy," he says when I just stare at him. He has a flat Midwestern accent, and his voice comes out a little pinched, like air escaping a punctured tire.

"I know it's your booth, Bo. It's your booth every goddamned morning."

"Do we know each other?" He's somewhere between puzzled and pissed. For a big guy, that voice is high, and does his tough guy stance a disservice. I wonder if it cut into his effectiveness as a cop. I wonder if he's been battling it his whole life.

"You don't know me, but I know you."

"Listen, if this—"

"Shut up, Bo. Shut up and use your ears. You're going to have the opportunity to open your mouth again, and when you do, I want it to be to tell the truth."

"I don't—"

"Who paid you to look the other way on March 25th?"

He blinks once, twice, swallowing hard. He's a headline in large type, as easy to read as the newspaper in front of him. "I don't—"

"I'm going to describe your sister's house to you, Bo. It's on Wilmette Avenue, about thirty minutes from here, a white clapboard two-story number with a green mailbox out front. Your nephew, Mike, occupies the bedroom in the upper right corner and your niece, Kate, right? She sleeps in the lower left below a pink Hannah Montana poster. Your sister, Laura, she's been living alone now for what? Two years?"

Bo's face turns bright red, like a brake light. His voice rattles now. "I don't know who you think you are—"

I cut him off. "I'll tell you. I think I'm the guy who will kill your sister, your niece, and your nephew in the next hour if you don't tell me exactly what I want to know. And when I get done killing them, I'll head to your parents' house in Glen Ellyn. The brick number set back from the street with the two-door garage? Eventually I'll come back for you, Bo."

He starts to open his mouth, but I'm quicker. "I know you were a cop. I know you still have friends on the force. But I'm going to tell you as directly as you'll ever hear anything in your life: you and your friends have never dealt with someone like me. There's already a file on your family that will read 'unsolved homicide' if you don't tell me exactly what I want to know."

He lowers his eyes, and I've got him. I growl through clenched teeth, "Who paid you to look the other way?"

For a moment, he doesn't say anything, just pushes waffle crumbs around the table. Then, so softly I almost don't hear him, "Not look the other way . . ."

"Speak up."

"Not look the other way. He paid me to leave. To get up and head out. Said he'd only need an hour. Gave me two thousand bucks. I didn't know what he was up to, I swear."

"What'd he look like?"

"White guy, little dumpy to tell you the truth. Shaved head . . . just a regular guy, you know?"

"Accent?"

"I don't know. East Coast, I'd say, but I don't know. He didn't say much. Just said 'two grand, walk away, one hour.' That was it. He handed me the money and I took off, you know? I don't need any Mafia trouble if you know what I'm saying. Cooled my heels in Sharky's down the street. Looked at my watch and the hour was up. Gave it an extra half hour just to make sure I didn't walk in on something I didn't want to see. But when I came back, everything was the same."

"Video?"

"That was the thing. Of course, I looked over the last hour's video. Or I was going to. But it was all erased, like the hour didn't happen. I don't even know how to work the console other than to hit rewind and play, but he knew how to do it. And there was nothing there."

He shakes his head, remembering. "I held my breath the next day, expecting to hear about some big theft, but nothing. No one ever complained, and no one came to me and said anything illegal happened, so I just . . ." He glides his hand out like an airplane taking off and says, "pssssh."

"Until today."

"Yeah." Now he looks up and meets my eyes. His expression is resigned, like a kid caught stealing, sitting in the store manager's office, waiting for his parents to show up and mete out some punishment.

I stand, and he can't help but exhale, relieved. Curiosity gets the best of him, though. "So what was taken?" He looks up with expectant eyes.

I don't answer and head for the door.


"So that's why you had Smoke put a file together on the security guard." I had asked him to do so a few days before, and he had come through quickly. The file was green but not bad; it contained what I needed to make an effective threat.

Risina walks next to me as we move north up State Street. We stop in a sporting goods store, and I move to a rack of ball caps.

"Yeah. Like in most businesses, information is key. The more you have, the more specific you can get, the more effective your threats are. What you have to do is plant images in your mark's mind and let the threat spread like a virus. Let his imagination do the job for you. You don't have to be particularly intimidating, you just have to know a few pointed facts about his family, about their names, about their houses, and the mark wilts like a picked flower. That's what a good fence does . . . gives you the information that gives you the power."

I pick out a blue Cubs hat and then move over to women's clothing where I select a pair of baggy warm-ups and a large, plain T-shirt. "Try these on."

"You're shopping for me now?"

"Until you figure out how to blend in a little better, yes."

She looks over the clothes I hand her, wrinkles her nose, and heads to the changing booths. If she thought being a female contract killer meant leather pants and stiletto heels, she's learning the opposite now. That shit looks good on a silver screen, but'll get you killed in Chicago.

After a minute, she exits, and it's all I can do to keep from laughing. Her hair is tucked up under the cap and the clothes fit like a kid trying on her dad's softball uniform. But the effect works: it's impossible to see what kind of a body she has under the clothes, and with the cap lowered, the top half of her face is in shadow. It's not perfect—you don't want to go too far the other way so that someone thinks "why's a beauty like her wearing dumpy clothes?"—but it'll do for now.

Archie's office is in an old aluminum manufacturing plant on Harrison. Risina, Smoke, and I sit in a conference room, a stack of files on a long wooden table.

"This is everything, Smoke?"

"All the files in the last six months, plus a few Archie was putting together."

"Okay, each of us takes a third. Sing out if you read anything that jumps out at you."

"Meaning?"

"I don't know. We're tracking breadcrumbs looking for red flags. I don't know why someone wants to find me, so we have to work off the assumption that Archie's abduction is a factor. There are plenty of ways to try to find someone, but they chose to rough up Archie, which makes me think there's a personal connection between the kidnapper and him. Maybe it has something to do with a hit he fenced, and usually these types of things are immediate, so I thought we'd narrow it down to the last six months. He keeps thick files. Just look for anything that . . . anything that looks abnormal. That's the best I can think of to do to get started."

Risina nods as Smoke divides the folders and slides her a stack. If she's surprised by the amount of professional killings contracted in the last six months just by this one fence, she doesn't show it. I think I know why. Here is something she can relate to, something in which she excels: literature. She opens the first file and burrows into it like a mole. I watch for a moment, thinking about that first time I saw her on the Via Poli in Rome, surrounded by all those austere books. This is a different kind of reading—a long way from Dickens and Walpole and Dante—but compelling just the same. After a moment of watching her, I pull a file off the top of my stack and get to work.

The first few files are typical assignments: eight-week jobs in various corners of the country. One shooter was assigned to each, and the jobs were all completed on time. Nothing remarkable about the marks: a lawyer, a construction contractor, a horse jockey. Guys who had no idea death was coming for them until the moment their bells were rung.

The fourth file is interesting. Archibald used one of his contract killers—a woman named Carla—to settle an old personal score back in Boston. Archie took down a rival fence who had set him up on an aiding and abetting charge.

"Tell me about Carla?" I say to Smoke.

Smoke shrugs. "Dumpy woman. Nothing special. Archie borrowed her from another fence, wasn't in his regular stable. I don't think she worked much. Burned out or got burned or something."

"You ever meet her?"

"I did. On that job you're holding now. She needed a scrounger to get her a bunch of equipment, and I helped facilitate."

"What's a scrounger?" Risina asks.

"A fella who gets you any props you need while working a job—a delivery truck, a uniform, a wheelchair, an ID badge . . ."

"Weapons?"

Smoke shakes his head. "Your fence'll supply those."

"Yeah, scroungers are mainly for everyday things. They get paid well to work quietly and quickly." Then, to Smoke, "What was your vibe off Carla?"

Smoke shrugs. "Not much to look at. Had a dog-face if you want me to get specific. Not sure what breed, but definitely canine. She didn't say much either, all business. A little jumpy, to tell you the truth. Why? What's in the file?"

"Nothing . . . just . . . a personal gig for Archie. File says it went down the way it was supposed to go down. It shouldn't be suspicious; but if I were looking for a reason to kidnap a fence, I'd start with the jobs he instigated himself. I might want to talk to this Carla."

"Archie didn't have a problem with her. Like I said . . . that was the only time he used her."

"Okay."

I set the file aside and plow into the next one. An hour goes by with no further anomalies, no red flags waving at me. Shaky clients called off a few hits before the assassinations took place, but this is not uncommon. Clients buckle under the weight of what they've set into motion, and they'll pay extra to cancel the order, trying to salvage their conscience, afraid to wake up with blood on their hands. Fences can make a pretty good business on canceled hits.

I just open the last file in my stack—the execution of a pit boss at Harrah's Casino in Joliet—when Risina speaks up.

"I think I found something."

And she did.

It's rare, but occasionally in this business there are incomplete hits. Not canceled hits . . . incomplete ones. An assassin might get killed while on the job, or the mark goes into hiding and just can't be found, or the police or FBI catch wind and sting the bagman in the act. The fence is forced into an awkward position; he has to turn the money back over to the client, which is a substantial sum, half of which, subtracting his fees, he paid to the hit man on commencement of the assignment. So personally he's on the hook for the total, unless he can barter with his hired gun to return a portion of the commencement fee. If his hired gun is alive and not in jail, that is. Worse, the fence takes a shot to his reputation by failing to execute the assignment. Clients get jumpy, rival fences swoop in like vultures to fill the void. A few dings like that, and the contracts dry up.

Four months ago, Archie put a file together on a Kansas City man named Rich Bacino. This is the file Risina found, the file I'm absorbing now. On the surface, it doesn't look like a difficult kill. Rich started an internet software company in the boom of the nineties and was prescient enough to sell it before the bust of the aught-years. He netted eighty million dollars before he turned forty. A bachelor, he bought up properties on both coasts and added an apartment in Paris. He spent a little money on the usual accoutrements of the rich: cars, boats, real estate. But Rich saved the majority of his cash for a newfound passion.

Rich started collecting.

Over the years, I've seen a lot of marks involved with an assortment of illegal activities. I've killed crime bosses, money launderers, numbers runners, low-level bagmen. I've killed corrupt politicians or judges taking bribes on the side. I've hit businessmen with mistresses and Sunday school teachers who were buried in gambling debts. I've also come across a few assholes involved in illegal collecting: kiddie porn or Nazi memorabilia or stolen art. You dabble with that stuff, it's just a matter of time before a guy like me shows up on your doorstep. You sit in slime long enough, you make enemies and you get dropped.

But Rich's collection is a first.

Rich Bacino collects skulls.

He has over fifty, all famous people, all acquired after the bodies were laid to rest without the heirs or families knowing about the exhumation. DNA tests and documentation prove their authenticity, though very few people will ever see the paperwork to confirm it. Collections like this aren't gathered for display; it's hard to describe, but they're built on a perverse sense of getting over on everyone else. It's like Poe's telltale heart beating underneath the floorboards while the constable stands obliviously above it—except instead of driving the collector mad, the beating, the *knowing* excites him. While his friends, family, and acquaintances visit in his living room, they have no idea that the skulls of say, Ronald Reagan or Jeffrey Dahmer or Gianni Versace are stored in the basement beneath them. It's a big secret fuck-you to everyone, an "I'm more powerful than you'll ever know" high.

Exactly how much he pays for the skulls, I have no idea. Archie estimates millions of dollars exchange hands for each purchase. The more famous the person, the more public the grave, the higher the price.

So Rich either crossed someone he shouldn't have, or someone's loved ones found out about his hobby, because a price tag was put on *his* skull. Archie was hired to facilitate the kill, which was an eight-week job assigned ten weeks ago. And yet, Rich Bacino is still alive.

The bagman assigned to kill him was a native Chicagoan named Flagler. Next to his name, Archie had written a single word in red ink.

Missing.

I don't know if this odd file has anything to do with the abduction of Archie or the note asking to bring me home, but it's an unresolved issue in Archie's professional life, and it seems like a good place to start.

# CHAPTER THREE

Risina and I are eating burgers at Blackie's on South Clark. The joint has been here for most of a century, and in a town that knows how to cook meat, it's a standout.

Smoke settles in across from us in the booth, looking a bit twitchy.

"What's up?"

"Nothing. I'm just not good at this, is all."

"You did solid work on the security guard."

Smoke shakes his head. "That was a piece of pumpkin pie. This . . . I don't know if I helped much. I wish Archie were here." He takes out a file and slides it furtively across the table.

I put my hands on top of the manila envelope but don't open it, just level my gaze at Smoke. "Give me the highlights."

"Well, looks like we've used Flagler twice before this job, but Archie didn't know him too well. Like that Carla you mentioned, he wasn't in the regular stable. He came on a rec from an East Coast fence named Talbott."

"That who you talked to?"

"That's who I *tried* to talk to. He gave me the Heisman." Smoke strikes the trophy pose before dropping his hands back to his lap.

"You gotta work him . . ."

"I don't have the tongue Archie has . . . you've seen that."

"I think you're selling yourself short."

"Man, I don't know."

Risina pulls the file out from under my hands and starts skimming it. "There's a lot of solid information here, Smoke."

Smoke shrugs, his eyes downcast. "I need a cigarette. Excuse me." He climbs out of the booth and heads for the exit.

Risina starts to read the first page in the file, then stops. "You don't think Smoke . . . ?" She pauses, trying to figure out the best way to say it. "You don't think someone maybe got to Smoke, do you? Or that he's been involved from the get-go? I mean, this note says to bring you to Chicago, and here you sit."

I shake my head. "I think he needs to find his footing. Gain some confidence. This job is . . . it's not for everyone. It's one thing to watch Archie put files together, another to get out and beat the streets all by your lonesome. I'm sure I rattled him in that alley in Manila. Maybe he's putting one toe in the pool and finding out the water's a little too deep. Being a fence is a lot harder than it looks. Psychologically, I mean."

"Hmmm." Risina goes back to reading, her eyes floating over the page. I like the way she's thinking now, even if I don't agree with her. She's starting to engage her intuition, a weapon as important to a hit man as his gun. She's asking the right questions, at least.

After a moment, Smoke returns to the booth, smelling like his namesake. "Sorry 'bout that. I tried to quit smoking once, but that didn't work out for me. Anyway, while I was out there I was thinking there was a nugget I found in this Flagler file that stuck with me. It's in there and you'll come across it, but I'll tell you anyway. This cat didn't pick up his money himself. Both times, the commencement pay and the completion— he gave instructions where to drop it. Now, most of Archie's regular guys on the payroll, Archie pays 'em direct. They're tight, you know? They're . . . like I said before . . ."

"In the stable."

"Yeah. Not this guy."

"You know where the drop-off was?"

"Yep. I took the duffel myself. Trailer park goes by 'Little Arizona' near the Indiana border."

"And you handed it to him?"

"No, that's the thing. I never met him."

Smoke's file gave me part of Flagler's story, but it had holes in it big enough to drop a body through. He started as a bagman in Maryland, Virginia, and DC, and stayed mostly in that area up until about a year ago. Smoke didn't know what he looked like . . . and if Archie did, he didn't put it in his file. Archie was good about keeping notes on all his contractors, but for some reason, hadn't gotten around to recording much on Flagler. Smoke was sure *Flagler* wasn't his real name, but didn't know where, when, or why he chose it.

There was scant information regarding the jobs he'd worked on the East Coast, just that he had a fence named Spellman who died of colon cancer, allowing Flagler to become a free agent. He must've pulled a few jobs for the other fence named Talbott, who gave the recommendation to Archie, but like Smoke said, Talbott wasn't talking.

What Smoke did find were details on the two jobs he pulled for Archie prior to the one that went sour.

The first was the owner of a bar in Minneapolis, a sixty-year-old lothario. From the file Archie cobbled, the man was juggling six different women in various parts of the city. Three of them were married. I have no idea who ordered the killing: a jealous woman or a cuckolded husband, but the barkeep's Don Juan lifestyle caught up with him. He was shot in his car at one-fifteen in the morning after he closed down the bar and put his key in the ignition of his Cadillac. Robbery was the police department's initial suspicion; the safe inside the bar's back office was open and empty. But as details of the bar owner's social life emerged, the police shifted their attention to his spate of lovers. A dozen people were brought in for questioning, but all the suspects seemed to have strong alibis. The case remains unsolved and open.

The second assignment was a bit of a high-profile case. It involved the violent death of a professional athlete. Again, Flagler used the robbery angle to throw the police off the scent. This is not an uncommon tactic; hired killers have been utilizing it for centuries. Make it look like a petty theft gone wrong and the cops will spin their wheels for weeks, staking out pawnshops and flea markets, trying to find the killer by tracking what was stolen. All the while, the trail grows as cold as a frozen pond. Robberies are supposed to be about money; the goods *have* to be fenced at some point. So nothing drives a detective more insane than when the stolen items simply vanish.

In this case, the athlete was a cornerback for the Bears, a guy who mostly worked on the punt and kick-off teams, but occasionally made it on to the field in nickel packages or long-yardage situations. He was in his sixth year in the league, and hadn't made a fortune, but had done all right for himself. He lived in a decent-sized house in Cabrini and was into guns, amassing dozens of handguns and rifles.

He was shot in the foyer of his house, just inside his front door, while wearing a bathrobe. He lived alone and his body wasn't discovered until he missed his second day of practice. Most of the athlete's weapon collection had been stolen from the home, and the police went the robbery/homicide route.

The cops staked out gun shows and various shops around the city, but none of the weapons ever surfaced. Flagler was smart enough to bury them in the woods or drop them in the bottom of a lake, making the stolen guns a trail that would only lead to frustration. Half of a bagman's job is to escape cleanly after a mark is hit. A good killer's best weapon against the police is to behave illogically.

Contract killers know how homicide cops think. They want to keep their "closed" case percentages up, and nine out of ten murderers are handed to them on a silver platter. A boyfriend kills his lover. A husband kills his wife. A drug dealer pops his rival. A couple of days of work, someone cracks, someone steps forward, and the homicide is solved. Case closed. A contract killer has no personal connection to the victim, and if he's good, he makes it look like the intention of the killing is something it's not. When the case goes infuriatingly cold, it's human nature for a homicide detective to move on to greener pastures.

Despite Smoke's misgivings, he had given me quite a bit to go on; in fact, Flagler's *modus operandi* helped fill in the blanks on why he went missing.

Flagler was contracted to kill a man who owned a strange, expensive collection of human skulls. I think Flagler finally found something worth stealing he didn't want to bury.

Little Arizona is located in Hegewisch, smack between Powder Horn and Wolf lakes, on top of an old landfill near the Indiana border. For being so near the city, it's a rural lifestyle, where fishermen can reel in a blue gill or a carp, and hunters can legally bag birds seeking a drink as they migrate south. For a trailer park and despite the occasional meth head, it's not a bad life.

I left Risina and Smoke back in the city to do further research on Flagler, to see if the two of them could sift through the silt of Archie's files and pan out any more gold. Risina was content to examine more of Archie's work, and didn't protest when I told her I'd like to make the run to the drop site alone. I have an ulterior motive for leaving her behind though: this is the first time I believe I might head into some violence, and I don't want to expose her. Not yet. Whether or not the violence is going to be directed toward me or dispensed by me doesn't make a difference.

The park is quiet and the plots for the trailers are spread out wider and more haphazard than I imagined, like someone dropped a box of matches and just left the sticks to lie as they fell. A black curtain of clouds is gathering in the north and heading this way, and I'd like to scope out the site and uncover any salient information before the skies open. Rain, so often thought of as a blessing, a life-giver, the washer of sins, is no friend to a hit man. It causes fingers to slip, vision to blur, and muddy ground to hold shoe prints in clear relief. Best to get in and get out before any complications.

Smoke had dropped Flagler's money off at the white and green pre-fabricated home in plot number 73. He said that both times, a middle-aged woman answered the door, took the duffel bag, and closed it in his face without saying a word. It's odd for Flagler to use such a method for receiving his kill fees . . . if he didn't want to collect his money himself, why use an immobile—rather than a fluid—location? Why use the same drop site twice?

When a lion is looking for a kill without having to expend too much energy, he follows the hyenas.

I knock on the door and paste a pleasant smile on my face, ready for the inevitable glance out the nearby window. After a moment, the door opens, and the middle-aged woman Smoke described grimaces down at me. She has meaty arms and a fleshy face, but with a layer of hungry menace in her eyes, like an alley cat who has found a home and no longer has to fight for its daily meal, but still keeps its fur up all the same.

"What'choo want?"

"Flagler."

Her eyes flash for only a moment and then she leans into the frame, looking down at me. "You ain't gonna buy it when I tell you I don't know no Flagler?"

I shake my head.

"I figgered. What'choo want with him?"

"I want to talk to him."

"Well, if you find him, tell him I'm looking for him too. I haven't seen him in months."

"How do you know him?"

"How does anyone know anyone?"

"You have a picture of him?"

"Wouldn't that be something. No . . ."

"All right then." I start to leave, waiting for her to make the next move. Before I get ten steps from the door . . .

"You sure you jes' want to talk?"

I turn. "Well, I have something for him, but I'd like to give it to him myself."

"What?"

"None of your business, ma'am."

"Money?"

I let her digest my hesitation. "That's between me and Flagler. If you see him, tell him I'm staying at the South Shore Inn on South Brainerd."

I head for my car and make a show of driving off.

Less than ten minutes later, she is in an old Celica hatchback that looks like it might roll over and die at any minute. She speeds out of the trailer park, tires throwing up dirt and gravel as she maneuvers on to the highway that cuts around the lake. The car is painted white and stands out nicely against the blacktop. Even as the rain hits, I can track it as easily as an elephant in short grass.

I settle in, not sure how far she's going to drive. She isn't making any evasive maneuvers, happy to roll down the highway like a homing beacon. I'm content to follow the hyena.

Forty-five minutes on the road and her blinker glows red as she exits into Edison Park, not far from O'Hare. Killers often live within a stone's throw of an airport, not just for convenience while on a job but for escape when things grow uncomfortable.

She parks in front of a hardware store, lumbers out of the Celica and hurries inside. I wait for a moment, gnawing on my lower lip. I thought she was going to break for his residence, so this detour to a retail shop has thrown me off. Does Flagler work here? Or more likely, own the place? Or is it a front for something else?

Five minutes have gone by and no sign of the hyena. I'm just going to have to go in after her. I'm starting to feel like the tables have flipped, and maybe I'm not the predator but the prey. Damn it, she just wasn't smart enough to pull it off, to bait me into the spider's web, was she? So why am I climbing out of my car now, exposed to the rain, heading toward the stand-alone store with the red awning marked, "Wayne's Hardware"? Why am I in Chicago anyway, the moment someone puts my name in a note? If I've lost a step, I'm going to pay for it.

As I move quickly across the street, a new thought bangs around inside my head: *I'm glad Risina isn't here.*

And that's the crux of what has been dogging me since we left Manila. *I'm glad Risina isn't here.*

Can I do what I do and protect her? This moment, this situation reinforces that interrogative like the question mark at the end of the sentence. Should I force her to see it my way and explain it doesn't have to be the end for us? I know I'm not going to watch her die and I know I'm not going to leave her unprotected if something should happen to me. Not even a week into this assignment—I'm already thinking of it as an assignment, even if this is a rescue operation instead of killing someone—and the folly of the two of us working this as a tandem sweep starts to appear like cracks in a foundation. The question looms: is it better to recognize that folly now than to stand face to face with the ramifications under worse conditions?

Focus. Fuck. The hardware store has display windows in the front, the kind that let shoppers know of sale items but don't offer a view into the store. I quickly check the sides and the back but no windows. Only a gated rear door and a rolling receivables dock allow access into the place from the back alley. The neighborhood isn't the friendliest in Chicago and the proprietor has gone out of his way to make his shop impenetrable after hours. I guess I'm just going to have to waltz in the front goddamn door.

From the best I can gauge, the entire store is maybe three thousand square feet, but I don't know if it has low shelves so you can see across the length of it, or high shelves like a maze, or if the cash register is in the front or the back or how many workers or customers or . . . goddammit, I'm just going to have to play it like it lies, get my head on a swivel, keep my eyes peeled, and be ready.

I keep my gun tucked into my back since it's raining and I don't know if I'm walking into a store full of customers or a fortress full of killers, but my hand is at my hip and ready.

I throw open the door and nearly bump into the hyena before I can take one step inside the store. The woman gets a panicked look on her face and bellows, "He's here!" a split second before I wallop her in the side of the head, dropping her like a stone, but her warning's enough, and whatever element of surprise I had evaporated with that shout like boiled water.

My eyes still haven't adjusted to the light and I hear the distinctive rack and eruption of a shotgun, a thick BOOM, BOOM. I jerk my head straight down on instinct and paint cans explode in the spot I vacated.

A double-barrel can be effective at close range but not from forty feet and it's a bitch of a gun to reload, and so I charge in the direction from which the cartridges were fired, my Glock leading the way, hoping I can stop him before he cocks the weapon again, and as I dash up the aisle, I just barely catch a flash of a red shirt barreling toward me, closing the distance, both of us with the same idea in mind. Before I can brace myself, he drives into me like a bull, sweeping me off my feet. We collide into a three-tiered shelf filled with paintbrushes, toppling it on top of us. I don't know where my gun went but it's not in my hand.

Even though the hyena came to warn him, I must've caught Flagler off-guard, unprepared, because his only line of defense was a shotgun and once both barrels fired, he resorted to grappling. I'm guessing she fed him the bit about someone with money asking around for him, someone who was staying at a motel nearby, and instead of realizing she'd led him right to me, he prepared to go on the offensive. Maybe I should have let that happen, played possum, rope-a-dope. Maybe that would've been better than lying on my back unarmed in an aisle of scattered paintbrushes.

He must've been taught somewhere how to street-fight. Before I gain my bearings, he goes right for my eyes, clawing with his fingers, trying to rake my lids with his nails, and when I move my arms up to block him, he immediately switches tactics, heads south and tries to pound my groin.

With all that time in a juvey home, I've learned a few dirty tricks myself, and flip my hips before he can land a sapping blow. Undaunted, he leaps up and off me. The high ground is always a good position to take, so I'm expecting him to try to stomp down on me but the blows don't come and when I look up, he's taking off for a different aisle.

As quickly as I can, I find my feet and sprint after him. Whatever he's going for, whatever he has stashed in this store, a hardware store for Chris'sakes, can't be good. The hyena is making mewing noises near the front door and if any customers with cell phones decide to come shopping right now, it won't be long until the cops are right behind them. I'm hoping the rain will keep them at bay. Who wants to look for lightbulbs and wingnuts in this shit?

I spot Flagler halfway down an aisle, and when he turns to face me, he's two-fisting a sledgehammer, the old fashioned kind with a steel mallet attached to the end of a hickory stick. I set my feet and prepare for the inevitable rush.

Before he makes his move, though, he wants to talk.

"What do you want?"

"Whatever you took."

This causes a genuinely puzzled look to spring to his face. "What're you talking about?"

"Rich Bacino. You were supposed to kill him but you didn't."

His eyes flit now, like he's trying to calculate my play.

"What's it to you?"

"I think you took something from him instead. I think he either bought you off or you stole something out from under him. That's your play, take some shit so the cops think it's a robbery. Only this time, you took something worth a lot. And Bacino wants it back."

"I don't . . ."

"Whose skull did you steal?"

His eyes narrow. My question landed. I can see it working out in his brain: does he try to deny it or just charge me?

The latter wins out and he raises the sledgehammer like a baseball bat, rushes in and swings in an upward arc, a homerun swing, a golf swing, aiming for my head. I duck backward and the mallet catches the shelf to my right, knocking it down and only too late do I realize this was also part of his feint. He released the tool as soon as he swung it, never really intending to catch me with it, and instead bum-rushes me while I'm still spilling backward, off-balance.

This time he crouches low and drives his shoulder into my sternum, lifting me off my feet so I can gain no traction before he pile-drives me into the cement floor.

Flagler is better than I thought, a professional hit man who is strong even without a gun in his mitts. He knows how to work over a body, knows how to get his knuckles bloody, and as I absorb the blow and try to keep air in my lungs, I start to think maybe I'm going to lose this fight, maybe he's better than I am. Maybe after all this time, it won't be a gun that brings me down but a brawl. I lost a few steps in my layoff and a man who never left the game is knocking more than my rust off.

He's hammering my ribs with his fists and I can't take much more before my wind is gone and then both of us hear the rack of a gun's chamber, my gun, and I twist my head to see the hyena, pointing the gun our way, terrified, out of her element, about to squeeze the trigger, trying to plug me while I'm on my back and compromised.

It's the distraction I'm looking for. I buck Flagler up as the hyena closes her eyes and squeezes the trigger and the gunshot is ear-splittingly loud as it echoes off the cement floor. The bullet catches Flagler in the upper arm, sending him sprawling. An amateur firing a Glock almost always hits a spot a couple of feet above the intended target as the pistol's kick is much stronger than anticipated.

She opens her eyes and her face blanches as she realizes what she's done. Before she can correct her mistake, I kick her legs out from under her, take the gun right out of her hands as she tumbles on to her back, and then drive an elbow into her nose, popping it and punching her lights out a second time. That crack should keep her down for a while.

Flagler does what I would have done . . . he tries to scramble away. I catch him easily and drive a fist right into the wound, and as he bites on that pain, his hand comes up in a feeble attempt to cover the bullet hole. I drive a second punch into his fingers, *through* his fingers, and he sprawls out on the floor, submissively throwing his hands up like a white flag.

After I do a quick search to make sure he doesn't have any blades stashed in his clothing, I move to the front door, flip the "closed" sign around and lock it. We're going to have a longer conversation now, and I'm reluctant to share it with any new arrivals.

Flagler lives above the hardware store. It's a bizarre front for a professional hit man. Most killers prefer to deal with the public as little as possible, but here's this guy, welcoming them in and selling them circular saws and ceiling fans.

"My pop owned this place for forty-two years," he offers by way of explanation. "He left it to me when he croaked and I figured what the hell, I'll keep it open. He was a decent dude. Never did me wrong. She does more business than you'd think. Got to where I was only taking one or two contract gigs a year after I moved back. Should've just quit the game entirely. I definitely thought about it."

"Who's the drop girl? The one who shot you downstairs?" I didn't really care, but I liked the way he was Mr. Chatty all of a sudden.

"My aunt Elaine. Elaine McCoy. I used to call her the Real McCoy because she always kept it real with me, you know? You didn't end her, did you?"

This guy. I shake my head once. "Hogtied on aisle six."

"The rope aisle."

"Yep."

He nods, "Thanks for that. She knows what I do, and she knows she's in it, but still, it would've been a shame."

"Where's the skull?"

"You gonna shoot me after I tell you? I don't care much, I'd just like to know if it's coming so I can get my mind right."

I shake my head again. If he's relieved, he doesn't show it. If he doesn't believe me, he doesn't show it either.

"There's a floor safe under the lamp there. Combo's 24-34-24."

I look over in the direction he indicated. "You open the safe, fish out the skull and give it to me. Afterward, you can call whatever doctor you use and get 'im over here. I wasn't hired to kill you, so I'm not going to do any pro bono work. I just need the skull."

He walks stiffly over to a straight black floor lamp near a television. Using his good hand, he rolls it along its base and exposes a recessed safe before he stoops over the lock. His face is white from the bullet wound; sweat has broken through and drips off his forehead. He forces himself to concentrate as he twists the dial on the safe's face, and then exhales when the door pops open.

I put the barrel of my pistol up against the middle of his back as he reaches inside with both hands. In movies, guns at close range are always pointed at victim's heads, but the head is the easiest part of the body to jerk suddenly, like I did when I heard the shotgun cock downstairs. But the middle of the back? The middle of the back is damn near impossible to spin out of the way in the time it takes for a skilled gunman to squeeze a trigger.

He doesn't flinch as he withdraws a bone-white human cranium from the safe and hands it to me.

"You gonna ask me whose skull it is?"

"I'm gonna ask you something else."

"Yeah?"

"What would've happened if I would've dialed 24-34-24 into the safe like you told me?"

He swallows. His face blanches as white as the skull bones.

"I . . ."

"You told me 24-34-24. But when you popped open the safe just now, the combination you used was 10-20-10."

He smiles weakly. "You caught that?"

"Yeah. I have good eyes. Could've been a fighter pilot."

He shrugs. "It . . . uh . . . it would've blown up in your face."

"I figured."

"Does that mean . . ."

I fire into his back twice, through his skin and into his heart. He flops forward, dead before he can finish the sentence.

I wasn't lying when I told Flagler I wouldn't kill him. But attempting to trick me into tripping a bomb puts a foot on the throat of my mercy.

# CHAPTER FOUR

I walk into the warehouse, and for the first time, I realize I'm soaking wet. The cool air hits me as I step through the door, and I shudder as though a ghost walked on my grave. Like I said, though I haven't been on an assignment, not really, it *feels* like an assignment. The tiger is a tiger, and though some may forget, may think of the animal as domesticated, as tame, the beast remembers what it is, and watches, and waits. Instincts, though dulled, are resurrected like Lazarus. Smiles turn to screams. Familiarity turns to non-recognition. And love? Love inevitably turns to grief.

I played the game against a worthy opponent for the first time in over a year, and I came out on top. A feeling is growing inside me I'm not sure I can contain. I'm not sure I *want* to contain it.

The tiger is a goddamned tiger.

Risina has her back to me when I enter, and maybe she feels a change in the air, a charge, like an electric current ripping through the walls, because she bolts upright, nearly over-turning her chair as she spins.

"You scared me," she says breathlessly. Her eyes find what's in my hands. "Is that . . . ?"

I nod at the skull, holding it up like the gravedigger in Hamlet.

"You know whose it is?"

I shake my head, and she laughs. The sound is like a hypnotist's snap, a bell ringing, because whatever foreboding premonition I brought into the room disappears in that sound. That laugh, that look on her face, that simple prism in her eyes sustained me through so much it almost seems surreal, absurd, that I questioned going on without her.

And maybe that's it, what I haven't been able to get my head around until now: maybe the key isn't absence but proximity. Maybe the key isn't sending her away, but pulling her closer. Maybe Risina is my battery, my power source.

"So we make the exchange with Bacino? That skull for whatever information he has on why your name is involved."

"That's it." And she's touched on the biggest problem in all this: if Bacino just wanted his skull back, and kidnapped Archie to get me to do the dirty work for him, why would he cite me specifically? It doesn't add up, it's not simple, there's a piece missing. That's the way of the killing game: it's a messy business.

"I'm looking forward to meeting him," Risina says. Then, a second later . . . "Archie, not Bacino."

Smoke strolls into the room, his eyes downcast, his hands fidgety. I liked Smoke when I first met him, and I chalked his nervous disposition up to being a fish out of water, but now I'm suspicious. There's no doubt the time I spent out of the game dulled my skills; maybe it dulled my senses as well. I feel like a diver coming to the surface after a long time in the deep.

"Something wrong, Smoke?"

He meets my eyes, then quickly looks away, his head bobbing like a chicken looking for seed. "Nah, just anxious is all." I think that's all he's going to say, but he adds, "I swear I feel like I'm being watched or followed or some shit."

"You mark anyone? Same car in two different places, same eyes in a crowd, even if the face is different?"

Smoke shakes his head. "Nah. I don't think so. Like I said, I'm anxious. Wanna get this over and done with. Get Archie back. It was just a feeling, was all. Maybe I been drinkin' too many sodas or some shit."

I watch him twitch some more, like he doesn't know where to put his hands, so they stay in perpetual motion.

"In this world, you gotta trust your instincts, Smoke."

His eyes shoot up and search mine to see if there's any malice behind my words. Am I talking *to* him or *about* him? Am I challenging him? I don't give him anything, my face as unreadable as a cipher.

There's something he's keeping from us, something that has him as skittish as a deer, and I'm sure Risina spots it too.

"So now we wait for the meet, I s'pose," says Smoke.

"No."

His eyes shoot up again. "No?"

"Uh-uh. Playing defense is how you get backed into a corner, how you end up broken or dead."

Risina offers, "We take the fight to him?"

"That's right. Word of what happened to Flagler won't hit the streets until tomorrow at the earliest . . ."

"What happened to Flagler?"

I look at Risina carefully, and the question dies in the air.

"Oh," is all she manages and her cheeks color. I have to remind myself how new she is to this life. It's another crack in the wall of my plans to keep her close, but that laugh. I have to concentrate on that laugh.

"So we hit him tonight before he has a chance to plan for our arrival. We meet him on our terms. If Archie's alive and Bacino has him, we'll get him back."

Smoke nods, seeing it. He raises his eyebrows, and it looks like he's genuinely relieved. "I s'pose you want to see the original file on Bacino again."

"Yeah, we should all go over it and figure out the best place to hit him."

I like to confront a man in his bed. It's the second most vulnerable place to hit a target, short of his shower or bath. It is where a mark's defenses are at his lowest—even if he's stashed a weapon under a pillow or beneath the mattress, the added effect of being groggy cancels any advantage. The romanticized notion of a hunted man sleeping with one eye open is bullshit. Once a mark is down for the night, it is exponentially easier to put him down permanently.

I don't need to kill Bacino; I just need him to know how easy it is for me to get to him. I need to embarrass him. I need to make him regret summoning a hit man named Columbus.

According to the file made up for Flagler, Bacino lives in a mansion in Highland Park. He's alone, except for a half-dozen bodyguards, the occasional woman, a pair of dogs, and his older brother, Ben, who collects a salary but does little to earn it. Ben is supposed to be some sort of chef, cooking for his brother, but the file mentions his real job is a gofer, an errand boy. Groceries need rounding up? Ben does it. Coffee needs brewing? Ben does it. Car needs a wash? Ben does it, but not much more than that. Whether or not he knows Rich collects skulls is not mentioned in the file. They live on opposite sides of the house, and Ben is a foot shorter and a hundred pounds heavier, so I'm not worried about confusing the two.

The bodyguards live at the house and rotate out, two-two-and-two in eight-hour shifts to cover the clock. The guys are ex-cops or ex-military, and they indicate Bacino isn't trifling with his detail, isn't just trying to create an exaggerated sense of security the way some people put security company signs in their yards even though they never turn on their alarms.

Archie's file is a good one, and if he makes it out of this alive, it'll be at least partly due to his meticulous work. Bacino sleeps in a second-story corner bedroom that faces away from the street. He usually stays up late, hitting the pillow around midnight and then sleeping through the morning.

"I'm going to get to him at two a.m., wake him up from sugarplum dreams by tapping my Glock to his forehead. And Risina?"

She raises her head, expectantly.

"You're coming with me."

Outside, the moon is down and the sky is starless, as black as tar. We parked ten blocks away and hoofed the distance, both wearing dark shirts and pants. We stand in the expansive back yard of Bacino's neighbor, a Persian oil billionaire who is only in this country two months of the year. He pays a man to check on his property twice a day, but the caretaker cut that down to twice a week when he realized no one reported to the Persian about his performance. Risina and I have the yard to ourselves.

"Are you sure?" she whispers at about ten minutes to two.

I make certain she can see my eyes, even in the darkness. "You were in it with me, even before you knew you were in it. And if something should happen to me, you're still in it. You understand?"

"I understand. You told me it was your choice to have me here, but it is my choice as well. Yes?"

"Yes."

"The more prepared you are, the better I'll feel."

"Then let's go wake up Bacino."

We scale the brick wall separating the two yards as easily as steeplechase horses and stick to the shadows as we approach the back of the house. Archie's file is accurate: the night-shift bodyguards have joined up on the front patio to have a twenty-minute smoke. I imagine they've spent the last four years smoking together like this without incident, swapping stories about their lives away from this house, catching each other up on their wives or children or what the Cubs did the day before. I have a feeling they won't have these jobs much longer.

The alarm is a standard 10-zone system from a generic manufacturer, and since Bacino has a pair of golden retrievers who have free rein of the house, I'm confident he doesn't turn on the motion detectors. The sensor makers always say pets under forty pounds won't set 'em off, but they're full of shit. I'll know in a moment if I'm right.

We enter through a small rectangular pane of glass embedded in a set of French doors that lead from a den out to the pool. I don't break the pane—some alarms trigger just from the sound of glass shattering—so instead I use needlenose pliers to scrape away the wood putty and take out the glazier's points, starting at the center of the frame and working towards the edges. I only have a few minutes and have to move quickly. Once I pull the bottom of the wood apart, I gently slide the glass panel out and place it against the house. After we shimmy through the opening, I replace the wooden frame so to the casual eye, it looks like nothing is missing, though the pane is no longer there. The air is still, so I'm not worried about a breeze giving away our entry-point.

We sneak through an entertainment room, then a foyer, where we can just make out the soft voices of the two guards jawing away, and then we take a set of stairs to the top of the house before heading for the corner bedroom.

I feel Risina freeze even before I understand why, and then I hear the panting of a dog's breath, or two dogs' breaths, as I now make out their silhouettes in the doorframe of the nearby guest bedroom. They move forward, toward us, cautiously, their tails down, their ears pricked. If Bacino thought he owned guard dogs, thought they might bark a warning against intruders, he should have raised a different breed. Risina turns her hand palm upward and I do the same, holding it out toward the timid retrievers. Grateful for the acknowledgement, they mosey over and start licking our hands. A few quick pats to the head and they trot back to the guest room, mollified. Risina's grin is unmistakable, even in the dim light of the corridor.

As promised, I tap the barrel of my Glock on to Bacino's forehead. "Tap" is probably the wrong word; I pop him hard. He bolts up like a snake bit his face and the first thing he sees is Risina at the foot of his bed. I wanted to disorient him and she does a hell of a job at that. He blinks a few times like he's still trying to swim to the surface, and then I slap him between the eyebrows again so he jumps, clamps his hand over his head and barks a sharp, "No!" Not "stop" or "don't," but "no." Under the circumstances, I think it's a decent reaction.

I rack the Glock so he knows there is a bullet in the chamber and a second "no" dies in his throat. He starts to open his mouth, but I interrupt. "We have what you want . . . you need to give us back what we want."

"Who are you?"

"Columbus. Now where is Archie Grant?"

His eyes do that unmistakable thing where they squint as he searches his memory.

"I don't . . ."

I smack the hard polymer of the gun down on his nose. "Ow, goddammit . . ." he manages as his hands flock to the spot.

"A bit harder and your nose breaks. And I'll pop it right through your fingers if you don't start talking."

"Let me finish my goddamn sentence then," he croaks, his voice muffled by his hands. I don't look over at Risina to see if she's startled by my aggression. She hangs in my periphery, immobile.

I nod and Bacino continues, his eyes watering. I gotta give him credit for keeping the tough-guy act going under the circumstances. Hell, maybe he *is* a tough guy. "Mrs. Hauser. Kindergarten teacher. Craig Captain. Father's friend from college. Met him one time, when I was seven. John Mayfield. First man to ever cut my hair."

He dabs his hands near his nostrils to check for blood, but his fingers are clean, and then he scrunches his nose a few times. His voice remains pinched. "I have a thing for names. I remember names from before I could read or write. Guys I met only once. Guys my father brought around for a beer after work. Some people never forget a face . . . I never forget a name. Now you said this name, Archie Grant, like I should know it but I don't. You can pound on my nose until there's nothing left, but I don't know that name."

He's telling the truth; it's unmistakable. How does he not know the name of the guy he kidnapped? There is only one answer. Bacino's a lot of things, but he's not the guy I'm looking for.

An idea starts to form in my mind. Maybe I got the end of this story right, but misread the beginning.

"You missing a skull?"

His eyes flash. "Missing?"

"No one's stolen one of your skulls?"

"I . . ."

"You made a deal with a contract killer named Flagler." It's not a question.

He looks back and forth from Risina to me. "I . . ."

"He came to kill you, and you bought him off with a skull from your collection."

Now he doesn't protest or stammer, just lets me continue my train of thought.

"He doesn't put a bullet in you, and you promise to give him one of your most expensive, rarest items. That's how it went down, right?"

Bacino folds his arms across his chest and pouts. "I knew it wouldn't end there."

I reach into my pack and pull out the skull, the one I thought was swiped by Flagler but was actually traded to him by Bacino. A skull for a life. Bacino looks at it with the eye of a practiced collector.

"Do you know how much that's worth?"

I shake my head.

"More than the contract on my life, I can assure you. You got it, you keep it. I know I'm not in a position to bargain, but I'll make the same deal with you I made with the other guy. Don't kill me and that skull's yours. You can make a fortune off of it. It's the head of—"

And right then, his brother opens the door holding a leather collar and wearing only a bathrobe. "What talent you got up in here, bro?"

He's wearing a dopey grin and it takes a moment for his eyes to move from Risina to me. I can see the slow calculations take place in his head. He moves from lustfulness to confusion to understanding in the span of five seconds.

Good fences can get into a lot of places, discover a wealth of personal information, chronicle a life to a surprising degree. A pay-off to a talkative employee, a search through police records, a disguised visit to relatives or friends can prove indispensable in fleshing out a mark's file. And in areas that are off-limits, behind closed doors, an experienced fence will make educated assumptions.

Nothing in Bacino's file suggested he shared his late-night trysts with his sad-sack older brother. I thought we'd have another ten minutes before the bodyguards finished their smoke break, but now I understand why the guards take that break in the first place: to give these bastards some breathing room while they screw whores together. Who would want to listen to a pair of assholes slipping it to some one-night stand each night?

"Get help!" Bacino screams. It takes Ben a few seconds of blinking for the words to process. Then his lids pop open and his eyes widen as the pieces come together.

In a fistfight, the guy you're trading blows with will often try to land a haymaker to the jaw. The punch starts from somewhere near his belt and is as easy to spot coming as the headlight on the front of a train. An experienced dirty fighter will duck his chin and crouch so that the punch connects with the top of his head, almost always shattering the bones of the punching hand. It is the hardest part of the human body, the top of the skull.

Before Ben can flee, I hurl the stolen skull at his face with everything I have. The top of the cranium connects with his forehead, making a sound like a baseball bat thumping into a wooden support beam. Immediately, he drops to the floor as his legs turn to jelly.

Spying an opening, Bacino launches out of the bed and heads for Risina, roaring like a lion. I'm not going to be able to close the distance before he gets to her, but I'm going to make him sorry if he harms her in any way. He leaps for her throat, but she swings the gun around like she's unleashing a pair of brass knuckles, not taking the time to aim and pull the trigger, but nailing him in the side of the face with everything she has, the steel and polymer of the gun's barrel leading the way.

The blow connects with an audible crunch, a pistol-whip, and though it doesn't knock him out, it stuns him and shatters a few teeth in the process. Enraged, he blinks away tears and tries again, but I finish what Risina started, swinging for the back of his head with the butt of my gun, once, twice, until he falls face-down on the wooden floor.

The older brother Ben starts to groan.

"Time to go . . ."

"But?"

"He doesn't have Archie."

"You believe him?"

I nod and that's all she needs from me. We're out the door, down the stairs, through the opening and over the wall before the bodyguards tamp out their cigarettes. We'll get a few more minutes as they mistake the moans of pain upstairs for something else. It'll be all we need.

# CHAPTER FIVE

**A**ccidents don't exist in this business. A hit man dies, a fence goes missing, a mark wanders off the side of a building on his way to plummeting ten stories: none of this is surreptitious. This trade places a premium on precise planning, on exacting detail, and if a player has his ticket punched, more likely than not, a malevolent hand, not an act of God, is behind it.

The wind has grown belligerent throughout the day, racing around corners and smacking pedestrians in the face like a schoolyard bully. The sun is nothing more than a condemned man held in chains by a wall of dark gray clouds. The sky might rain, or it might just threaten the act, as though it gets some sort of twisted pleasure out of withholding the information. Every now and then, Chicago, as a city, likes to rise up and remind its citizens she won't be pushed to the background, she won't blend in behind them, she's a leading character in their life story and they'd be wise not to forget it.

The three of us, Smoke, Risina, and I, hurry under the scaffolding of some Gold Coast remodeling project and head toward a simple eatery named the Third Coast Cafe. "Pardon our progress" signs have spread across the city like kudzu. Everywhere I look, another building constructed in the late-19th century aftermath of the Great Fire is in the middle of a facelift. After the housing crash, all those construction workers had to find something to do with their time, so the city funneled stimulus dollars into the hands of no-bid general contractors. Of course, it wouldn't be Chicago if evidence of kickbacks and greased palms hadn't already been hinted at by the *Times*.

The workers swarm the scaffolding like wasps, the wind only a nuisance. They raise equipment, bang away at walls, scrape, sand, and plaster, ignoring the weather. I guess anything becomes routine if you do it long enough.

The restaurant is half-full this time of day and customers hunch over coffee and pieces of pie, reluctant to give up their table and head back out into the wind. We slide into a booth in the back corner and order some food. Smoke's nervousness has reached a new apex; his leg shakes up and down like a piston.

"We're in a jam now," he says. "We're up against it."

"Yeah, we're at square zero. We haven't even reached square one. The skull collector was an anomaly in Archie's files, but not the one who nabbed him or wanted me."

"We chased the wrong dog up the wrong tree."

"I suppose we could take a look at the file again, see if we can figure out who the client was, see if he's upset the mark is still alive."

"Seems like it wouldn't have nothing to do with you, though?" He's asking more than he's telling. He has a point, but his fidgeting grows even more exaggerated.

"What aren't you telling me, Smoke?"

When Smoke looks up, I can't tell if he's surprised by my question or if I caught him by being direct. He swallows and wipes his mouth with his napkin. He looks to Risina for help, but she gives him a hard stare I didn't know she had in her. I'll admit it's disconcerting, coming from her. I wouldn't want to be on the receiving end of that look.

"What'd'you mean?"

"You've grown more fidgety than a prisoner walking toward the hangman."

"I told you, I'm nervous 'bout this whole thing."

"Yeah, you told me."

"You know . . ." he tosses his napkin down on the table, then points his finger at me, "this is exactly what I was worried about. *Exactly.*"

"What're you worried about, Smoke?"

His finger hasn't left the air. "This! You turning on me, everyone looking at me like I had something to do with Archie disappearing. You think the first thing that crossed my mind when I saw that ransom note wasn't 'uh-oh, you stepped in it now, Smoke?' I've been scared shitless since he was taken, and I could've run a thousand times. Hell, I didn't even have to come find you; I could've just caught the first bus to Frisco and forgot the whole damn thing. But I did because Archie said if he were ever in a pinch that's what I was supposed to do."

His eyes focus, like he just now realizes his finger is jabbing the air toward me, that his voice is growing louder. He lowers his finger but doesn't lower his eyes.

"Let me tell you something about Archie and me. You won't understand this and I don't care if you do, but this is the truth and if that's a sound you've heard before then you'll recognize it now.

"I was twenty-eight years old before anyone believed in me. My whole life was spent with people telling me I wasn't good enough, wasn't smart enough, wasn't strong enough, wasn't solid enough, you know what I'm saying? My mom thought I looked like my father and never forgave me for that, even when I apologized. Can you imagine? Apologizing to your mom for the way you look? And all you get for it is your mother trying to beat your father's face off your neck.

"School stopped for me when I was fifteen. Just walked away and didn't go back. You think there were officers out there checking to see where I was? You think the school board or the principal or the teachers came around asking, 'why isn't Leonard in school?' Let me let you in on a little secret: they don't care. No one gives a shit. Just one more drop-out, one more black boy out of our hallways, out of our detention hall, and good riddance.

"My first arrest was for boosting a car. I'd love to tell you a story about how some buddy of mine talked me into it, or how I wasn't going to do nothing but drive that car around and forget my life for a few hours, but that'd be a lie and you're here for the truth. The truth was I knew that Cam's Motorshop out by the airport would pay a couple thousand to strip down Hondas with no questions asked and that's where I was heading when I got stung. I wanted the money, plain and simple. I turned eighteen exactly three days before my arrest so I did a hundred days at Cook County instead of juvey. That was about as much fun as a punch in the dick. I'm sure you've seen your share of hellholes but you have no idea. You have no fucking idea, I assure you.

"The second time I got picked up was across state lines. I had grown pretty skillful at jacking cars by then and I had a regular thing going with six or seven chop shops all over Chicago. This one cat named Holmes I worked with a few times asked if I could drive a hot Nissan over to Boston where his brother Todd had a shop and drive back some other wheels to Indy. Said he'd pay five gees for the trouble and that cash sounded pretty damn good to me. I don't know what I was aiming to buy at the time, but I remember that the money would set me straight for a while. Needless to say, I saw the bubble lights go up behind me just crossing into Massachusetts, and I panicked, ended up with a helicopter spotlight over my head, six cruisers, and a set of those spikes stretched across the road to take me down to the rims. It was like a Hollywood movie except missing the ending where the good guy gets away. Or maybe I wasn't the good guy, come to think of it.

"Anyway, state lines is state lines and I ended up in Federal without a friend in the world. I tried to call Holmes and I'll be damned if the number done changed. I was staring three years in the face and the Fed House meant organized crime and drug traffickers and El Salvadoran gangs and Aryan brotherhoods and a whole mess of hard cases who wouldn't think twice about putting your insides on the outside of you if you know what I'm saying.

"The second day I'm locked up . . . the *second* damn day . . . I get sucker-punched in the walkway between the chapel and the restrooms. I'm walking along and WHAM! on my back, laid out flat. Didn't see the fist fly, didn't see the face, just a blast of pain, blinking white lights, and I'm looking up at the ceiling. I don't know who hit me or why they hit me or what I had to do to make it right . . . no one tells you that shit. Look at me, I'm all of five-ten and skin and bones and I was even thinner back then if you can dig that. No one helped me up and no one told me what the fuck I was supposed to do to keep from getting jawboned again.

"When I went to get my meal that afternoon, I saw some of the prisoners snickering at me and my fat lip and my purple cheek but I just ignored them best I could and sat down at one of the tables they had scattered in the cafeteria.

"That's where Archibald Grant found me, busted lip and busted flat, eating a dry hamburger in the cafeteria at Lewisburg.

He asked me my name and he asked me my story and I don't know why I let everything out, but like I'm doing here, I did for him there. The words just poured out of me like water out of a busted bucket. I told him where I came from, where I'd been and why I was stuck up inside there.

"He looked at me, smiling that half smile of his, the way he does, you know, and didn't say nothing for a while. Then, he nodded like he'd known my story before I told it and he said I'd been stealing the wrong things. Cars, electronics, wallets, knicks and knacks, this place was full of people who boosted the wrong shit. Boosted it because they didn't know better. All that crap could only get you a little cash and what was the point in that? Risk versus reward was all upside down. Five thousand dollars worth five years in lockdown? In Federal? With these animals? Hell no. No fucking way."

Smoke shakes his head vigorously, then swallows hard. He doesn't look at us, lost in his story, as he continues.

"Archie folded his hands and lowered his voice. He said what he stole, the only thing *worth* stealing, was information. He said there was no greater commodity in the world. He said people laid down their lives for it since the dawn of man and they did it for good reason. Told me he stole information on the outside and he'd been stealing it on the inside, riding out his two-year term in comfort and security until he could resume business on the other side of the wall. Said he got thrown in here on purpose anyway, and though that claim had just the slightest ring of bullshit to it, I bought it like a fifty-cent bottle of beer. Looking back now, I'll just bet he did get himself thrown in there for whatever reason made sense at the time."

I remember that time. My old fence Pooley went to visit Archie in that prison, and commented how he couldn't get to him to put a scare in him, get the information I needed at the time. Maybe Archie was in there to avoid my reach back then.

It doesn't matter . . . I keep my mouth shut and listen to Smoke unfold his story.

"Anyway, I naturally said something along the lines of 'why you telling me this?' And he said, 'nobody ever believed in you, but I see a spark inside you maybe no one else saw before. Maybe it's buried deep down in there but I can see it.' Of course I thought he was completely shining me but fuck if those words didn't sound like honey. Say what you want about Archibald Grant, but he's got a mouth on him that could sell scissors to a bald man. He told me he knew who waylayed me in the hall outside the chapel and he knew how to take care of that situation so I wouldn't be bothered again, not even looked at askew the whole time I was behind bars, but I needed to do something for him. 'Could I do that?' he asked.

"I didn't know but I said I'd try. He said 'good, good.' Then he nodded to indicate a beefy prison guard standing behind the glass near the exit. 'See that hack over there what looks like he ate too many dollar specials at the Taco Bell?'"

Smoke stops and laughs to himself. "You know how Archie do."

I can't help but smile too, but signal with my hands tumbling over each other for him to get on with it. It doesn't do either of us any good to think of Archie in the past tense.

"He tells me the guard goes by the name of Nash. Archie says he's been able to crack the code on most of the hacks but this Nash has been a problem. Says he's tightlipped and none of the other guards'll spill on him.

"Now, as you can imagine, most bulls take a handout here or there for favors, but not this Nash. He's straight as an arrow and there was no chinks in the armor neither. He's one of those true blue badges you hear about but never expect to see. And those are the dangerous ones. Because nothing can fuck up a connected con's plans like a hack who won't play ball.

Suddenly, you find yourself transferred to the wrong cell-block, or your pleasantries are confiscated, or you're eating at the wrong table in the cafeteria or worse. Balance of power is always a precarious thing in life, but in lock-down, it's hanging by tooth floss, I'll tell you that.

"Archie looks me over, and says, 'get me *something*.' 'What'd'you mean, 'something'? I ask back, and Archie gets that look in his eye he gets time to time that says 'I'm smarter than you think I am.' He looks down his nose at me and says, 'What have we been talking about? Information, Smoke.' He's the first one to call me that by the way cause I had this pack of Parliaments I pulled out and lit up in mid-conversation. That's the one good thing I'll say about L-burg . . . you can smoke inside that damn place. What happened to the world where we kicked all the smokers outdoors? Anyway, Archie keeps on, 'Anything I can use on Nash to get what needs getting. One week. You find me some A-plus information and all your problems inside this box disappear like bad dreams in the morning light. Consider yourself off-limits for a week . . . nobody but nobody gonna be in your business, I *guarantee* that. And don't forget something, Smoke. I believe in you.'"

Smoke fiddles with his unopened pack, turning the box over and over, occupying his hands. I have a feeling he'd like to pause the tale to step outside and light one up, but telling stories has a way of gaining a foothold on anything else you might want to do, planting its flag until it's over. He looks up at me.

"So what the fuck was I gonna do? I'm like three days into this shitbox and I'm going to find out information on a hack no one else has been able to procure? A bull with a clean certificate? How the fuck was I gonna do that? But those words were there, Columbus. He said 'em and I'll be damned if he didn't mean 'em. 'I believe in you.' Those words were like, I don't know, they had weight, man. You believe that?"

I nod and half of Smoke's mouth turns upward. His eyes start to shine, but he doesn't wipe at them.

"First thing I did was spend two days doing nothing but watching Nash. Marking his shift changes, seeing how he conducted himself, who he talked to, who he watched, hell, I even counted how many times he scratched his nuts. But there was nothing there. He just stood behind the glass and watched us with dark eyes.

"Now, he wasn't always behind the glass and that gave me a bit of hope. The bulls took various shifts, sometimes behind the glass, sometimes in the corridor outside the rec room, sometimes walking the block, and sometimes out in the yard.

"I watched him, I watched him, I watched him, and this cat Nash did not give me a goddamn inch. Believe that. I started thinking maybe he's a robot, like some android out of a space movie. C-3PO or some shit. Cons would try to talk to him and he'd just ignore their shit and give 'em a stare that stopped 'em cold.

"I was five days into my seven and I hadn't come up with jack squat. Not a plan, nothing. My mind was racing. Maybe I just make up a story and tell it to Archie, but what would that give me? Seemed like I might as well grab a shovel and start digging my own grave out in the yard. But damn if your mind don't play tricks on you in the box when you start running out of options. And those words were hanging over me the whole time . . . 'I believe in you.' I know it sounds corny as a holiday card, but I wanted that belief to be rewarded, made whole . . . that's the only way I can describe it. I wanted to justify his belief. This man I barely knew. Had only spoken to once.

"Then I saw an opening. The slimmest opening possible. An opening that would add some years on my sentence and would put the 'hard' into 'hard time' if I got caught.

"See, one thing I've come to learn about this job is you gotta look at things from a different angle. I was trying to shadow Nash and pick up on a mistake or a flaw or some way to get inside with him, but instead, I should've been watching where he wasn't. I didn't say that right. Let me explain.

"I noticed that the guards went into a locker room just off of A block when they checked in. Various guards would be in and out of there all day, Nash included. When he came in, he'd be wearing a pair of khakis and an oxford shirt, but when he walked out, he'd be wearing a different pair of pants and the blue dress shirt that all hacks wore, you know? It came to me then and there. I had to get inside that locker room and see if there was any clue, any *anything* he left behind in his locker when he went out on shift.

"So there it was. All my eggs in that basket. I only had a day left, and how the hell was I gonna get into that locker room? Prisoners weren't supposed to be out of A block at all, much less in the bullring."

Smoke holds up one finger and flashes me a smile. "Except one inmate. One guy, that's it. Little sawed off son-of-a-bitch named George Yackey. The Yack Attack, my ticket in. This con got the sweet gig of shining the bathrooms, sweeping the floors, picking up the dead bugs off the windowsills in the area called 'A Extension' but what the cons called 'the bullring' cause that's where the guards went for break and change. Yack was the only orange jumpsuit allowed back there, twice a day, to clean up the ring and make it look nice.

"Now understand, the bullring wasn't near the perimeter or even on the outskirts of the building, so it wasn't like you had shotguns trained on you or the hacks would think you were trying to escape if they caught you in there. In a lot of ways, it'd be worse for you, 'cause if you were in the ring unauthorized, the guards would assume you were trying to fuck 'em in some way. Steal from 'em or what-not. And here's a little fact about serving time no one talks about: if you make a legitimate attempt at escape . . . if you get caught climbing the side of a wall, or in a tunnel or gripping the undercarriage of a laundry truck as it drives off the site, the hacks don't beat the shit out of you. Hell, they're not even sore. They actually show you a little bit of respect. That's the truth! Don't ask me why it's so . . . best I can figure, they put themselves in the con's shoes and say, 'why the hell wouldn't I want out of this dungeon any way I can? How'm I gonna blame this poor fool for trying?' Sure, they'll throw you in solitary for a month and take away privileges for a year, but when you walk down the block, they'll give you a nod like 'not bad, you crazy son-of-a-bitch. Not bad.'

"So if I was trying to escape, I might've had a bit of lenience if I was busted. But caught in their area? Caught in the ring? Those bulls'll go to town on your flesh until they catch bone, I guarantee that. That's lesson time to them. Gotta teach a lesson, right?

"Anyway, I went to Yackey's cell and I told him I needed a favor from him. I kept my eyes square and my hands spread like this, so he'd know I was in the *askin'* position, not the *tellin'* one, you know? He looked me up and down like I was dirt going down the shower room drain. So I made a play I had no idea would take, a play out of desperation, but what was I gonna do? I said, 'Yack, let me tell you about your future. In the next day I'm going to be on the inside with Archibald Grant, and if you know what that's worth, then you should climb on my back now. Do me this favor, and we'll reap the rewards together. But if you choose to cross me, if you tell me to fuck off and go away, then put your money on the 'don't pass' line and we'll see what happens.'

"He thought about it for a long minute, maybe the longest of his life, certainly was of mine, and then looked up and asked me what I needed. 'Five minutes of your time tomorrow,' was my answer.

"I did my best to clean my jumper and shave my face and trim my hair and do everything I could to blend in, not stand out, not give the bulls a single thing that would call attention to myself if they happened to look my way as I approached the barrier between A Block and the bullring. Five minutes, I told myself. Five minutes, in and out, get something, anything out of Nash's locker and run like hell back to the block.

"Now every day from two to three, that locker room in the bullring was empty. I clocked this for two straight days and this was the only pattern I could find. It had something to do with the rotation or the way they marked their shifts, but not once did a guard enter that locker room between two and three, and point of fact, the entire ring was empty during that time, save for George Yackey and his mop and bucket.

"At 2:15 on the last day, I walked from A block bathroom over to that barrier. Now, Yack Attack told me he'd meet me there at that time, swipe the card, get me inside, and that was that. But I'll be damned if he wasn't there.

"Now I'm standing next to the door and if a bull walks out of the cafeteria or out of the gym, I'm going to be looking like a big orange sign saying 'this fucking con is up to no good.' And I'm sweating and under my breath I'm cursing ol' Yack, this passive-aggressive motherfucker who told me what I wanted to hear but really placed his bet on the other side and the sad thing is he was right to do so. By noon tomorrow, I'd be powerless and he'd still have his sweet gig, so why the hell should he do me any favors?

"I'm stewing for a good couple of minutes, trying to figure out my next chess move, knowing that I need to vacate immediately, get the hell away from this barrier and get back to my cell and figure out what the hell I was gonna do in the next ten hours to get my ass out of this spot, and then I see the door to the locker room open inside the bullring and Yack shuffles out and heads to the barrier and opens the door to let me inside.

"He mutters something about wanting to make sure the coast was clear and for me to get the hell on with it, and if I don't start moving instead of gawking in the passageway, he's gonna slam the barrier back in my face.

"I move like a jackrabbit, into the bullring, one, two, three steps and I'm through the locker room door, my heart beating so hard I can feel it in my throat, and there I was feeling as exposed and vulnerable as a naked baby.

"The locker room was pretty much what'd you'd imagine, sort of in the shape of a domino, two rooms really, a half partition in the middle, with rows of lockers along each wall and wooden benches in the center so the bulls could change their socks or whatever needed changing.

"The clock in my head was already ticking as I stood dumbfounded in that off-limits room, and it hit me that I didn't know which fucking locker was Nash's. What the hell was I thinking? Walking in here blind like this. I moved around the front room looking for a clue, but all the lockers were the same, just steel outsides, shiny and clean, no tape or nothing marking whose was which. Fuck me, my head was telling me to just bail out now, slip back outside and through the barrier before I catch a beat-down the likes from which men don't come back normal, but my feet kept moving me on. I was between a rock and a bigger rock, I'll tell you that.

"So my feet walk me into the back part of the room, and there it is, a mop set right up against one particular locker.

Yack Attack, who had no reason to do me any favors other than knowing I'd owe him if I did in fact find myself riding high after this, played me an ace. I moved the mop out of the way and even though the locker was locked, I slipped it open as easy as eating cake. I had one set of skills coming into this place and this baby lock wasn't going to stymie a man who knew his way around opening things up that needed opening.

"I get the locker unlocked and it makes more noise than I mean to make because I'm so fucking jumpy and my hands are a little sweat-soaked I have to admit, and I let the door slip and it bangs against the locker next to it. I hold my breath but no one comes a-calling, and I'm staring inside at his clothes, those same clothes I saw him come in with: a pair of khaki pants, neatly folded on a hanger, hanging next to a red striped oxford shirt and a blue blazer. Down in the bottom of the locker sit a pair of brown Cole Haan loafers. That's it. That's what I've risked my hide for . . . a set of clothes and nothing else.

"I fish through the pants pockets but they're empty, then I try the blazer but nothing in the inside pocket and I swear this headache springs up on me all of a sudden like when you drink something cold too fast, and I realize that my body's telling me emphatically and wholly that I've screwed the pooch and right then I notice some heavy coughing coming from outside the locker room door, like a fit, like Yack's out there choking on his lunch and through the murk of this headache I somehow realize this is a signal, a warning, and I shut the locker and dive behind the little half wall divider that separates the front part of the room from the back and press myself up against it as I hear the door open and a guard whose voice I recognize as this black bull named Propes is saying 'You okay, prisoner?' to Yackey as he enters the room.

"I got a fifty-fifty shot, that's all I got. Either his locker's in the back part and he's going to catch me there looking like a fish out of the tank or his locker is in the front part and I might, just might, be okay if I can keep my teeth from chattering. You know how many times your life comes down to such a clear-cut, fifty-fifty chance? Maybe five, ten times, and there it was: white marble and I'm okay, black marble and I'm gone, baby, gone.

"I hear Propes take five, six steps into the room and he's close enough I can hear him breathing through his nose the way he does, and my heart's beating now like a donkey kicking the inside of my chest, and the bull sniffles a few times and opens up a locker in the front room on the right, no more than twenty feet from where I'm hiding, holding my breath.

"I hear Yack say, 'you okay, boss?' and Propes says, 'just forgot my damn Advil,' and he must finally find the pills in whatever place he keeps 'em in his locker, because he closes the door and leaves without another word.

"Immediately, I'm back inside Nash's locker and I got one more place to look before I break down and cry, and so I stick my hand deep inside his shoes, and I'll be damned if I don't hit paydirt. He's got his wallet buried down in there and his keys and his sunglasses and some loose change, and I forget everything else and flip open the wallet. Forty seconds later, I'm out the door and Yack looks as sick with worry as I feel and another ten steps and he lets me out of the barrier and it is finished."

Smoke looks up at me and he knows he has me. I'm a sucker for a good story, and most guys in the game know how to spin one. Archie was one of the best and Smoke must've picked up a thing or two sitting beside him. I don't interrupt because I'm enjoying this tale and because I know he's telling the truth.

"Next day, next *morning* even, Archibald Grant shows up in my cell as soon as the bars open and this is what he says to me. 'Give me what you got.' Not 'did you get anything?' not 'tell me you didn't blow this, Smoke,' just 'give me what you got.' You see, he meant it when he said he believed in me. He knew I'd have something. He just knew it.

"I told him I had two things, actually. Nash's address on Las Palmas Street and that he had two little blond girls named Kahla and Mitty, ages 10 and 8, and that's all I could get. Archie smiled at me as big as Christmas and said 'even better than I thought, Smoke. Even better than I thought.'

"I'll tell you something, I don't know how he used that information to get over on Nash, but we've both been in this business long enough to know that if you got someone's address and you know his kids' names and what they look like, well, shiiiiiit. It don't take a mathematician to figure out what two plus two makes. Archie had that straight-shooting bull practically wiping his ass within a week. And Archie kept his word too . . . I didn't so much as have a con look at me sideways the rest of my time in Federal.

"Archie gained his release six months before me and I thought maybe that'd be my ass, but his grip on L-Burg stayed tight even after he shook tailfeathers. And the day I walked out of that cinderblock, he had a bus ticket waiting for me. Said I'd be working for him from now on and not to worry about nothing else. He said I'd still be in the stealing business, but stealing the most important shit of all: information. And he was right."

Smoke stands up and that finger comes up again. This time his lips quiver as he pierces me with his eyes. "That's my story. So don't sit here and tell me I had something to do with Archie getting kidnapped or that I might know who did it. Archibald Grant believed in me when no one else would. I'd give anything . . . check that, I'd give *everything* for him. You believe that, Columbus?"

I nod once. "I do." I can see Risina nodding too out of the corner of my eye.

"All right, then. Good. We on the same page and let's keep it that way." He picks up his pack of cigarettes. "I gotta go light one."

Smoke leaves the booth and heads to the front door.

Risina exhales as he rolls out of hearing range. "What do you think?"

"I think he gave it to us straight. What do *you* think?"

I can tell she's pleased that I reciprocated by asking for her opinion. "I think he's closer to Archie than you are, closer than I'll ever be. I think he's scared for his friend. I think he'd do anything to get him back. And I think he told us the truth."

I nod my agreement, pay the check, and Risina and I head for the door. I'm going to do something when I go outside that I rarely do. I'm going to apologize. Apologize to Smoke for doubting him. I need him with me on this, pulling in the same direction as me, and I need him to trust my decision-making, my instincts, even though those same instincts wanted to finger him as an accomplice or worse. The only way to accomplish that is to say I'm sorry.

Smoke is standing right outside the front door, under the construction scaffolding, his cigarette down to the filter, staring blankly across the street. I hold the door open for Risina and start to follow her outside.

Smoke looks our way, drops his cigarette to stamp it out, and his eyes search mine for, I don't know, understanding? Clarity? Acceptance?

I'll never know because the scaffolding crashes down like an avalanche, collapsing on top of his head, and kills him instantly.

## CHAPTER SIX

**W**e're in the kitchen, through it, heading out the back and I haven't let go of Risina's arm as I clench it in a vise grip. I only had a split second to react. I heard a sound like metal snapping and the whirr of a tension line releasing, all in the span of a crack of lightning, and as the scaffolding started to collapse, I shot my hand out, a miracle lunge, closed my fingers around Risina's arm and jerked her back into the café only a second before she would have been crushed. I didn't have time to warn Smoke, couldn't have shouted if I'd wanted to. The only thing I had time to do was watch him take the brunt of it, five stories of structure raining down on top of him like a machine press.

*Accidents don't exist in this business.*

Risina's natural instinct was to look back as the realization of what happened hit her. She wanted to help, to see if anyone could be rescued, to see if anyone was hurt but alive, but she's new to this world and I have to keep her moving, even if it means I bruise her arm because I will not let go.

Everyone hurries toward the front of the restaurant while we rush out the back.

"Wait, wait, wait," she's saying but I'm not waiting, not allowing her to break stride. A half block down the alley I finally loosen my grip and she practically falls over as she jerks her arm away.

"What're you doing?" she shouts. Her Italian accent kicks in when she's angry. "We have to see if—"

"We have to get out of here."

"But what if we can—"

"He's dead, Risina. I saw the structure come down on top of him."

"But how . . . how did it . . . ?"

"I don't know, but we need to keep moving—"

"It was an accident . . . we have to—"

"Listen to me! I told you when we started you have to follow my lead, and that's what I'm telling you now. We have to keep moving—"

"I'm not going to leave until—"

"That was no accident!" I say through clenched teeth.

My words hit her like an uppercut. Her whole face changes as the anger peels away. Her feet start up again and I don't need to grab her arm to lead the way. "What do you mean?"

"I mean it was supposed to come down on *us*."

We spill out of the alley onto Division Street and join a crowd that drifts out of a bar, then change our pace to match the jostling pedestrians, to get lost in them, and she doesn't say another word though I can see her face pulled tight in my periphery.

I don't think we're being followed.

Archibald Grant's office is deserted, but it won't be for long. Two forces are at play against us: word travels fast in this business, and power vacuums fill quickly. Some time in the next twenty-four hours, someone is going to find out Smoke died outside that Gold Coast restaurant. Without him around, a few of Archie's men are going to swoop in here like vultures and clean this place out, take the chairs, take the desks, take anything of value they can get their hands on and sell the lot to the highest bidder. The furniture isn't where they'll land the real money, though. Someone who guarded Archie or one of his bagmen will know the value in the files, the contracts, the information. A rival fence will pay handsomely for access to Archie's work, and some underling will soon attempt to provide it.

"So why are we here now?" Risina asks. "You want the files for yourself?"

"Not the files. File."

"I don't understand . . ."

I'm already ripping through the cabinets, looking for the stack Smoke slid over to me when we were trying to find an anomaly in the contracts over the last couple of years.

I had found an anomaly all right, but I didn't realize it at the time.

*Accidents don't exist in this business.*

"Help me find a file with the name 'Hepper' at the top. First name was something like 'Jan' or 'Janet.'"

We start pulling stacks out of the cabinet and blitz through them. I'm only looking at the names on the first page, the names of the targets. If it's not a match, I toss it to the floor and pick up the next.

None of the names in the initial stack look familiar, must not be ones I fished through the other day. I grab another batch and start flipping pages when Risina pipes up, "Ann Hoeppner?"

"That's it!" I say, more excitement in my voice than I meant. She hands the dossier over and I open the cover. "Yeah, this is the one."

Risina blows a stray hair out of her face and places her hands on her hips. "Can you please tell me what this is about?"

I hold up the file. "Accidents don't exist in this business," I tell her. And in a few minutes, to prove my point, I'm going to set this office on fire.

In the contract business, hit men employ various methods to kill marks. There are guys who specialize in long-range sniper rifles, guys who work in close with handguns or knives, guys who ply their trade with car bombs or poison or good old-fashioned ropes around the throat. There are experienced vendetta killers who'll carve up the target or take a piece of the body to bring back to the client, but Archie stayed away from that type of play. Vendetta killers leave an unseemly mess. Mafias like to contract these kinds of hits, but mafias have long memories and hold grudges. Archie knew it's best not to step into that particular sandbox unless you're prepared to get dirty.

But Ann Hoeppner's killer utilized a different method.

Ann was a thirty-eight-year-old college English professor in Columbus, Ohio. She wasn't married, had no kids, and lived alone just off the Ohio State campus. Normally, college professors don't make a lot of money, don't have fancy cars or houses, but Ann had a bank account that would make most Wall Street brokers buckle at the knees. Her grandfather had been a scientist and inventor whose most famous creation was the self-starter for automobile engines. When he retired, he held one-hundred-and-forty-three patents, owned two companies, and was one of the richest men in the Northeast. Ann gave her high school valedictorian speech in a crowded auditorium at the age of eighteen. She told her grandfather's life story to a bored audience, the exception being the ninety-four-year-old subject of the speech, who watched with moist eyes and rapt attention. He died seven days later.

When an attorney read the contents of the will the following week, everyone in the family was shocked to learn Ann was the sole beneficiary. Even as precocious as she was, the amount of the inheritance humbled and terrified her. Her parents, who had thought the old man senile, were genuinely delighted. Her cousins, aunts, and uncles were not.

Ann spread the money around to her extended family, though open hands were stretched in her direction for the rest of her life. She put most of the windfall into various investments and savings plans and bonds and retirement funds and went about her life as though nothing had happened. Sure, she paid for her tuition, room, board, and books, but never spent extravagantly. She drove a small SUV, lived on campus and ate in the dorm cafeteria. None of her fellow students knew she could have bought and sold the campus ten times over.

She wanted to be an English teacher and nothing, not even the kind of money that determined she'd never have to work a day in her life, deterred Ann from her goal. Nine years of school later, she received not only a doctorate degree but also an offer to teach at her alma mater.

Ann was in her tenth year of teaching when she died. The English building, Denney Hall, is a five-story glass and stone building on Seventeenth Avenue, not far from the football stadium. It has functioning elevators, but Ann liked to walk the stairs to get to her office on the top floor.

There were signs clearly indicating the stairs had recently been mopped, that pedestrians should be cautious, that the surface was slippery. The signs had graphics, too—the familiar yellow triangle accompanied by an exclamation point—"caution" it said. "Cuidado." But Ann must have had her head in a book (a common occurrence, and a conclusion the police quickly reached). At the landing between the third and fourth floors lay a copy of John Donne's sonnets. Next to the open book lay

Ann Hoeppner, a gash in her forehead and her neck snapped. She wasn't discovered until an hour after her fall. The death was ruled accidental after a cursory police investigation. Later, her estate was divided amongst her many family members—those same envious aunts, uncles, and cousins—as designated in her will.

But Ann Hoeppner's death was no more accidental than Smoke's. Her neck was snapped by a fall, but it didn't happen the way the police wrote it up, didn't happen because she had her nose buried in a book, didn't happen because she failed to pay attention to the caution signs placed at each stairwell entrance. A professional assassin named Spilatro, one of Archie's contract killers, performed the hit.

Like I said, bagmen use different methods to kill their marks, and Spilatro has a rare specialty: he makes his kills look like accidents. There has to be a direct line between this man's specialty and the way Smoke just died. Has to be. And I'm willing to bet you can connect the dots from Ann's file to Archie's abduction to the note that summoned me out of hiding.

"According to this, Archie used Spilatro three other times. Let's find those files and hustle out of here."

We locate two of the three before a large man enters the office through the front door. I have my Glock up and pointed his way before he can step another inch into the room. He keeps his hands in his pockets and meets my stare with blank eyes.

"Who're you?" he asks, his face unreadable.

"Nobody."

"Well, Nobody, what're you doing rifling through the boss's stuff?"

"The boss is gone."

He greets this news with the same disaffected expression. His eyes flit to Risina, but I won't look her way.

"You gonna put that gun down?"

"No."

He nods now, sniffs a few times. Despite his attempt to play it cool, I take the sniffs for what they are, a nervous tic.

"I think you and your lady friend best vacate."

"I think you better watch your fucking mouth."

Those words come from Risina, not me. Now I tilt my head around to look at her, and for the first time I see she has her pistol up too. I expect to see anxiousness on her face, but I see that she's sporting a half smile instead. It's unnerving for me; I have no doubt it's unsettling for the man staring down the barrel.

Slowly, he takes his empty hands out of his pockets and shows them to her . . .

"I apologize, ma'am . . ." he's saying, but she doesn't let him finish, interrupting—

"My friend and I are going to find the last thing we came to find and then you'll never see us again. Now you can do one of three things . . . you can sit in the corner and watch us until we go, you can leave and never come back, or you can make a play and see what happens. It's up to you."

I'll be damned if I don't break into a smile. The big man looks at her one more time, back at me, and then makes his decision.

"Don't shoot me in the back on the way out the door."

"Get the hell out of here." Risina waves at the exit with the barrel of her gun. The man takes a last look at us, then nods, turns, and doesn't look back.

As soon as he's gone, Risina blows out a deep breath, like a kettle holding the pressure at bay as long as it can before it finally releases steam. When I look over at her, she ignores me and resumes her search for the files. I can see her hands shaking as she sorts through the stack.

"You okay?" I offer.

"What do you think?" she answers flatly.

I know not to push it from there.

It takes another twenty minutes to find the final file. When we leave the aluminum factory, Smoke's office is ablaze because, like I said, accidents don't exist in this business.

We sit on opposite ends of a couch, our backs to the armrests, our feet intertwined, facing each other. A pizza box is open on the small, glass coffee table and Risina digs into her third slice. We're in a two-bedroom suite in one of those corporate hotels that rent by the month to traveling executives. Smoke set us up before we got here, and I'm almost certain the information of where we're living while we're in Chicago died with him.

"It's natural to be nervous," I offer as Risina polishes off a pepperoni.

"I know it is." Her response is matter-of-fact, as though she's already chewed on her flaw for a bit and decided to approach it clinically. "I thought I did a fine job of keeping it under control."

I agree, but I don't say so. Instead, I ask, "But for how long?"

"As long as was needed."

"And if he'd've rushed you instead of backing away? What would you have done?"

"He didn't, so I don't know."

"Would you have pulled the trigger?"

"I don't know. How should I know?"

"Because you need to already play it out in your head . . . decide what to do before it happens. You already have an analyst's eye and you're going to have to rely on that to see everything from all angles. Improvisation is a weapon too, but it's dangerous. Planning is key."

She starts to interrupt but I hold up a finger. "Planning doesn't mean you have to know everything before you walk into a room, though it helps. Planning means that as a situation emerges, your brain needs to immediately start calculating, 'if this, then that. If that, then this.' Rapid fire, as soon as it's happening.

"Take the guy today. He walks in unannounced, and you did the right thing, got your gun up and out and pointed in his direction before he could step a foot in the door. Put him on his heels and on the defense. It's like a chess match, you have to always be thrusting forward, on the offensive. But you can't just stop there; you can't think linearly. Immediately, your brain needs to kick in with . . . 'if he runs, I follow. If he pulls a gun, I shoot. If he bum-rushes, I shoot. If he wants to talk, I give him some rope.' All of those decisions at once, bam, bam, bam, bam, bam.

"Now by the size of him, I figured he was some low-level muscle Archie kept around for protection, but since Smoke wasn't there to tell us he was on the payroll, I wasn't going to take any chances. You follow me?"

"I'd follow you anywhere," she says with a mock-seductive intonation.

"It's an expression. It means . . ."

"I *know* it's an expression. I just like to see you worked up."

"Goddam, Risina . . ."

"Awwww . . ." she tosses the pizza aside and reverses positions so her body falls on top of mine. "I'm just having some fun."

Before I can protest, she cuts me off. "Kiss me."

"What?"

"You're warm. Kiss me. You can teach me how to act like a killer later."

And like with the man who walked into Archie's office, she doesn't leave me with much of a choice.

The three remaining files fill in some gaps on Spilatro. When he employs a new contract killer, Archie likes to first flesh out the file with information on the assassin himself, and then additional facts and opinions are added to the dossier after the initial hit is complete. Archie's sister Ruby once told me he put together a file on me, but I never asked for it, and he never gave it to me. Not that it really mattered. If it existed at one time, if it was in his office with all the others, it's nothing but ashes now.

Spilatro came to Archie as a recommendation from a Brooklyn fence named Jeffrey "K-bomb" Kirschenbaum, a brilliant and feared player in the killing business, a man who wrote the book on how middlemen conduct their lives. Kirschenbaum grew up Jewish in the Bed-Stuy portion of the borough, which toughened him the way fire tempers steel. A gangly white kid in an all-black neighborhood, he had to learn to maneuver like an army strategist from the time he was in grade school, figure out how to manipulate opposing forces so he was never caught in the middle. Let the black kids have their turf wars and street fights. Deduce who was going to stand at the top of the hill, and make sure his allegiance fell in line. He was smart with numbers, but even better, he was smart with information, and a word here or a note there could swing a rivalry in a direction that most benefited "K-bomb." He liked playing the role of the man behind the curtain, the puller of strings, and as an adult fresh from a short stint at CUNY, he found his way into the killing business, constructing a stable of assassins out of his old contacts from the neighborhood and running his new venture like a CEO. He pioneered the idea of doing the grunt work for his hit men, of not just accepting a fee and doling out assignments, but of following a mark, of putting together a dossier on the target's life, of setting the table for his hired guns to make their hits. It was a real service operation, from top to bottom, soup to nuts. He provided each gunman with so much information, the shooter could plot myriad ways of killing his target while escaping cleanly. Consequently, a number of skilled assassins sought him out for their assignments, and his reputation grew. He treated his men fairly, and after thirty years, he remains a towering figure in the game.

Archie knew him, and he had exchanged resources with K-bomb from time to time. Five years ago, when a client hired Archie to specifically make a hit look like an accident, Archie reached out to Kirschenbaum to seek advice about whom he should bring in for the job. K-bomb said he had just the man, and farmed Spilatro out to Archie for a percentage. Unfortunately, Archie didn't collect much more information on Spilatro beyond who his fence was. This sticks out to me, a bit out of character for such a diligent fence. It speaks to how much Archie trusted or looked up to Kirschenbaum. It's awfully hard to see clearly when we have stars in our eyes.

That first hit was on a news reporter named Timothy O'Donnell, who also happened to be serving on a jury at the time of his death. *The New York Times* reported that on May 6, construction scaffolding collapsed on top of the middle-aged man while he was jogging his familiar route through downtown. It seems Spilatro isn't afraid to use old tricks for new assignments.

The other two files present similar kills . . . a bookkeeper died of asphyxiation in a building fire, and a police detective had his ticket punched when he slipped on a patch of ice and froze to death, unconscious, in an alley behind his local bar in Boston. That particular job was worked as a tandem sweep: Spilatro and the same assassin who struck me as odd before, the woman named Carla who'd worked the personal kill for Archie. What role she played in this murder isn't mentioned, just that it was a success.

"Here's what's absent from all these files . . ."

"What's that?" Risina asks.

"Any personal information on Spilatro. What his real name is, where he lives, how he got his start, where he grew up."

"And Archie usually has that?"

"Yes."

"But no one knows any of that information about you, either."

"Except Archie did at one point. And someone else does now."

She starts to say something, then smiles. "Yes, of course. *I* know."

"So we need to find out if Spilatro has a 'you' in his life."

"I see. And how do we do that?"

"We go to New York and talk to his fence. Kirschenbaum."

"He won't want to give up that information."

"No, he won't."

"But we're going to make him."

"Yes, we are."

"And he's good at this. So he's going to be protected."

"That's right."

I take her face in my hands, one palm on each cheek, and put our foreheads together.

"If you don't want to do this . . . if you have any concern at all, I won't think less of you."

"Are you kidding? I think there's a bigger problem evolving that you need to consider."

"What's that?"

"I'm starting to like this."

# CHAPTER SEVEN

Ridgefield, Connecticut is an affluent, three-hundred-year-old neighborhood settled at the foothills of the Berkshire Mountains. It boasts an historic district, an art museum, a small symphony hall, and two private high schools. Some sixty miles from New York City, it's a simple, ninety-minute train ride from the Branchville Metro North station, conveniently located in the southeast corner of town, all the way to Grand Central Station in Manhattan. And yet, it is a world away from Bedford-Stuyvesant, or "Bed-Stuy."

Kirschenbaum lives on a knoll in a five-bedroom brick house on four private acres in Ridgefield with vistas overlooking half the county. He has no wife, no children, no ties to the real world to be exploited. His house is a fortress, and he employs a regular staff of professional bodyguards, top-shelf guys who know how to handle a weapon and don't rattle.

There are several ways to reach a man who doesn't want to be reached. Usually, I focus on vices since most people who dip their toes into this pool have a few secrets they want kept in the deep end. They'll visit whores or buy narcotics or have a thing for guns or want to diddle boys, and this gives me a way to get to them. But I don't have time to plan a successful sneak attack, and I don't have a fence to help me figure out and explore his vices, and with Risina along for the ride, guns blazing might not be the best approach either. Navigating this world over the years, I've learned there's a time to explode, loud and aggressive, and there's a time to be supplicant, quiet and introspective.

Risina and I approach the brick columns bordering the gate leading to Kirschenbaum's property. There is a callbox but no button to press and no cameras visible even though I know they are there.

"Tell Kirschenbaum Columbus wants to see him," I say to the gate. "I don't have the time or resources to go through the proper channels. I'll be in room 202 tonight at the West Lane Inn for the ten minutes following midnight. If men come through the door with guns out, those men will be dropped. I have no problem with Kirschenbaum; I just need information."

We turn and head down the path back to the street.

Kirschenbaum arrives on the hour and enters the room alone. If he's trying to set a tone, trying to signal he isn't intimidated, it works. I'm impressed. He doesn't need an entourage, doesn't bother with his retinue of bodyguards—he watched me on the tape at his gate and decided on this strategy, to come devoid of self-doubt.

From what I'd read about him, I knew he was tall, but his height is pronounced in person, or maybe it's accented by the way he almost has to stoop under the low ceilings of this old rustic inn. His hair is jet-black without a trace of gray, swept back from his forehead like he's wearing a helmet. He wears a tight navy sweater and black slacks. His eyes are pale, striking, alert. He has half of a robusto cigar jutting out of the corner of his mouth like an extension of his face, and the smoke hangs around his head like a wreath.

He stands just inside the doorway, and looks at me, seated in a wooden chair near the small table, then turns his neck without moving his body to pick up Risina, who hasn't moved from the corner near the door. I placed her there, in his blind spot, and she has her hands behind her back, leaning against the wall. A threat but not threatening.

"Where do you want to do this?" His voice is a lower register than I would have guessed. It seems to come from somewhere near his abdomen and has a raspy quality, like a frog croaking. He talks around the cigar like it isn't there.

"You want to have a seat?"

He heads for the only other chair in the room without nodding, sits and crosses one ankle on his knee, then folds his arms across his chest, comfortable as can be. After a moment, he takes the cigar out and holds it between his thumb and forefinger to use it as a pointer.

"She joining us?"

I shake my head.

He turns to her. "What's your name, darling?"

That's something we hadn't yet discussed, and I curse myself for not thinking to do it sooner. There is an art to a fake name, and we should have decided on one a long time ago, before we entered the country. I'm hoping she doesn't answer, but one thing I've learned about Risina, she rarely does what I think she'll do. I may not have thought of a name for her, but she has.

"Tigre," she says, not missing a beat, her accent thick.

I feel warmth rise up in my chest, though I keep my face blank. A tiger is a goddamned tiger. Since Smoke located me in that bookstore, I've thought *I* was the tiger, the hibernating predator who recognized the familiar scent of prey after a long lay-off. What I hadn't thought about, what I hadn't considered until just now, is that Risina, too, is a tiger. I'm not sure how I feel about this. Am I relieved she is more like me than I thought, or disappointed?

Kirschenbaum seems satisfied and spins back to me.

"You two working a tandem?"

"That's right."

"How can I help you, Columbus?"

"You know my work?"

"I've been following you since your early days with Pooley. I never met the guy but his reputation was solid. It's too bad he had his ticket punched. You were with Bill Ryan after that?"

"Yeah."

"Too bad about that one, too. And now Archibald Grant."

"Yeah."

"Anyone ever tell you you've had some bad luck with fences?" He says this matter-of-factly, and pops the cigar back in his mouth. I'm starting to understand how Kirschenbaum made such a name for himself. I feel like maybe I stepped under the ropes and into a ring, except we're going to spar with words instead of boxing gloves.

"That's why I'm here. Archie's been taken."

"I heard. That's why you approached my gate. Where I live. With no appointment. No warning. Just walked up to my front gate."

"Like I said, I want information."

He spins to Risina again. "Can you get me a glass of water, honey?"

She doesn't move, just smiles. He turns back to me, now grinning. He raises his eyebrows like he took a shot at shaking her, and no harm done. Then his face turns grave again. He's switching tones and moods and expressions so fast, it's dizzying.

"Information costs."

"It always does."

"What do you want to know?"

"I want to know everything about a contract killer you represent named Spilatro."

He doesn't blink. "I know quite a bit about him."

"That's good. Now I know we're not wasting each other's time."

"Here's a tidbit to wet your whistle. He doesn't do the work you think he does."

He's telling me this so, like any salesman dangling a carrot, I'll bite. Instead I duck his jab . . .

"Do you know his real name?"

"As sure as I know your real name ain't Columbus. And you're originally from Boston. And your first fence wasn't Pooley but a dark Italian named Vespucci. And . . ."

Fuck, is he good. He's jabbing, jabbing, jabbing, trying to stagger me. To throw him off his rhythm, I interrupt. "And if I were here to find out what you know about me, I'd be impressed, but I'm not, so I could give a shit. I want you to give up Spilatro."

"So you can kill him."

"Possibly."

"How much you guesstimate giving him up is worth?"

"You tell me."

"I'll take her."

He jerks his thumb over his shoulder at Risina. The air in the room cools instantly, like a chill wind blew in through the vents. He puffs out a cloud of smoke and watches me through the haze.

I narrow my eyes but otherwise check my emotions. I hope Risina won't react, won't drop her wall, but Kirschenbaum doesn't give her the chance. He brays out laughter, a harsh, barking sound that, like his voice, seems to come from deep inside him.

"You should see your face right now. Jesus. I'm just fucking with you. Something tells me if I tried to take—what'd you call yourself again, babe? Tigre?—something tells me if I tried to take her, Tigre would stick a knife down my throat."

"Try me," Risina says, coolly.

"Nooooo, thank you." He holds his hands up innocently, then turns back to me as his smile fades. "Two hundred thousand."

"How do you want the money?"

"Bank transfer. You have a cell phone?"

I shake my head. He fishes one out of his pants pocket, moving quickly and deliberately, not at all concerned that one of us is going to shoot him for putting his hands where we can't see them. He punches some numbers into the panel and then flips the phone to me.

"That's my accountant's number. Have your bank call him and work it out."

"Okay. Transfer goes through in the morning . . . I'll pick up the information on Spilatro tomorrow night. Where do you want to make the exchange?"

"I'm sure as hell not going to write anything down for you. You know where I live, so come on over and we'll pour drinks, clink glasses, and have a powwow. You're invited this time."

I flip him back the phone.

"Keep it," he says and starts to toss it again my way.

"No thanks. I'll remember the number."

"Of course you will, Columbus." He bolts up quickly and, without shaking hands, heads for the door. "Tomorrow night then. And like you said to me so colorfully, you come in with guns leading the way and you'll be dropped." He takes one last look at Risina and says, "That goes for you, too, honey. You mind if I call you 'honey'?"

"You can call me whatever you want as long as you give us what we're looking for."

"What part of Italy are you from?"

"The part that ends in an 'a.'"

He smiles at that—or it could be a sneer—shoots a finger-gun her way, turns the knob, and heads out, only a cloud of smoke left behind to let us know he was here.

"How'd I do?" Risina asks when we're sure he's gone.

"You're a natural," I say, and I'll be damned if I don't mean it.

Eight minutes later, and we're out of the hotel without checking out, leaving Ridgefield until tomorrow night.

After breakfast at an all-night diner, we hole up in a chain bookstore in nearby Danbury, a two-story anchor to a shopping center. The place isn't crowded this time of day, and a clerk with "Janine" on her nametag points us upstairs to the fiction shelves where we can get lost in the maze of bookcases, couches, and corners.

Risina flits among the titles like a butterfly, stooping over here or standing on her tiptoes there to read an author's name or a jacket blurb. She looks over the books, and I look over her.

*Why aren't I more concerned?* Or better yet . . . *why don't I feel guilty over what I've done?* I'm like a condemned prisoner who, instead of slinking off to a cell to live out his sentence, drags someone down the hole with him. I've lived sleeping with one eye open for so long, why would I ever wish wary nights and watchful days on someone else? But it's not that simple, and here's the part I have trouble admitting. This job is dangerous, yes, it is haunting, yes, and it exacts a moral toll, yes, but it also holds an allure that is almost impossible to understand until you've hunted a mark, ended his life, and escaped without a soul knowing you are the shooter. It's a drug, a high, a tonic. It's not a delusion of grandeur, because it is grandeur itself.

What I realize now is I want someone to share the experience with me. It's one thing to tell these details to a stranger, another to discuss everything with someone who is there, going through the same swings, the same highs with me.

Was I lying to myself when I justified bringing Risina along by saying she was already in the game so she might as well learn the rules? Or was I, once more, putting myself first?

"How much time do we have?" she asks, her finger inside a David Levien novel.

"All day."

"Good." She heads to an overstuffed chair at the end of an aisle, back to a faux-paneled wall, plops down, and starts reading.

Another answer is possible. The reason I found Risina, or maybe the reason she found me: she's been a tiger all along and only needed someone to unlock her cage. She's a natural. A predator.

And if that's the case, what happens when she first tastes blood?

The gate buzzes open, and Risina and I pull our sedan in and park near the front door. I'll admit, I'm troubled by the one sentence Kirschenbaum jabbed with: *He doesn't do the work you think he does.* I didn't know where he was going with that, but I didn't want to chase my tail either. He wasn't lying to me—he definitely knew something about Spilatro he didn't want to come right out and say. But what? *He doesn't do the work you think he does.* I did bite the carrot after all.

Smoke died in an accident the same way this contract killer operated in the past. I have the files that prove it. Spilatro killed Smoke, but he meant to kill me. He has to be the guy who put my name on the paper, the guy who kidnapped Archie. So why would Kirschenbaum say Spilatro doesn't do the work I think he does? What other work does Spilatro do?

Efficiently, Risina and I cross to the entrance and don't have long to wait as a mustachioed guard opens the door and points upstairs without saying a word. There's something familiar about him, but I can't place him and he has me wondering: did Kirschenbaum plant him somewhere else around us? Was he in the hotel? The bookstore? Have we been watched from the moment we left his front gate? And if this guy was trailing us and I didn't pick him up, then how many other men did K-bomb put on us? Kirschenbaum didn't have the career he had by flying by the seat of his pants, and maybe what I mistook for calm bravado in our hotel room was actually informed caution.

I've got a feeling of foreboding I've learned to trust over the years, but I don't want to look back at the guard and give away any hesitation, so I head up the staircase. Risina is in front of me and maybe that's what's making me jumpy . . . we've been on someone else's turf together before, but this is the first time that someone's known we were coming. My intuition told me that Kirschenbaum's play would be to give me what I want, that he's a bottom-line opportunist and the percentages were to give up information on Spilatro rather than risk a confrontation with me, but maybe my intuition is rusty and I'm going to find out I'm wrong the hard way.

We make it to a long hallway with wood floors and the first thing I notice is that the guard—where did I see him before?—didn't follow us up and, in fact, there are no other guards visible on the second floor. I know Kirschenbaum platoons his security but I don't know where they position themselves in the house, and the whole thing is starting to reek like a corpse.

Risina looks back at me for guidance. She knows instinctively not to ask questions aloud, and I nod her forward toward the cracked door that spills light at the end of the corridor. I think she picks up something on my face because she blanches a bit, swallows hard, and then keeps moving.

I'm acutely aware of our breathing, the only breathing I can hear in the house, and the front door opens and closes downstairs, I'm sure of it. What the hell are we walking into? If I could think of where I saw that guy, maybe without the mustache, maybe with different color hair or no hair, goddammit, I'm coming up blank . . . I can now glimpse a four-poster through the crack in the door, so this must be the master bedroom, and I touch Risina on the elbow to let me pass and enter first. She steps back and my heart pulses now, a welcome feeling, a fine feeling, and maybe Risina feels it too because she looks alert and spry.

The guard didn't frisk us, which is unusual but not unheard of in this situation, especially since we'd made contact and been invited here by the man we're meeting. I wouldn't have given up my gun anyway and we might have had a problem downstairs, but it doesn't matter now and I pull out my Glock from the small of my back and I don't look but I know Risina is doing the same.

Three more feet to the door, and there are voices, but they're television voices, two idiot anchormen blathering on about some reality star and that seems incongruous with the man in our hotel room, what he'd be watching on a weeknight, just one more square peg that doesn't fit. So much for not coming in with guns out . . .

I push the door open wider and the bedroom is empty, but there's an open set of French doors leading out to a deck on the right and maybe he's out there, but why wouldn't he have signaled us or had someone show us in?

This is not right and there's no use for pretense anymore.

"Kirshenbaum?"

No answer. As I move to the deck, I tell Risina to watch the door.

The deck has some patio furniture, the rustic kind of chairs with green cushions surrounding a slat-wood table, and Kirschenbaum is out here all right. He's wearing a plastic bag over his head, held tightly around his neck by an elastic cord, and his hands are tied behind his back and strapped to his feet. A lit cigar is in the ashtray in front of him.

I hear sirens in the distance headed our way and in that moment it hits me where I know the guard. I've seen him twice before, and goddammit, I should have recognized him. I used to be a fucking expert at breaking down a face, noting the eyes and the ears and the parts you cannot disguise, but I used to be a professional contract killer and now I don't know what the hell I am.

The first time I saw him was in a construction vest on scaffolding outside of the Third Coast Café, except he wore a dark beard and blond hair, and the second time was without facial hair, or any hair at all: the big bald guy who came into Archibald's office and asked us our business, the guy I fucking let go because I thought he was nobody important.

There can only be one answer. The man who let us in was Spilatro, and he's been playing me like a violin since I got to Chicago, or maybe before that, maybe since Smoke pulled a safety deposit box out of its slot and caught a flight to find me.

"What is it?" Risina calls from the doorway and I realize I need to snap out of it and move now if we're going to escape.

"K-bomb's dead."

"What?" she asks, alarmed.

"Spilatro's framing us. Let's go."

I take her by the elbow and just poke my head into the hallway when a pistol cracks and bullets pound the doorway next to my head. I feel Risina duck back and I spot blood fly and goddammit, if he hit her . . .

We spill backward into the room and her cheek is scratched to hell but not from a bullet, rather from splinters from the door and she looks angrier than I've ever seen her, like the blood on her cheek brought the tiger to the surface for good. Multiple pairs of feet pound up the stairs down the hall, and I catch a quick look at them as I fire a few rounds back, popping the first guy flush and stopping the rest, and maybe they don't know the boss is already dead, and maybe they don't hear the sirens as they close in on us.

Spilatro wasn't with them, though, I'm sure of it. The son of a bitch must've planned the whole thing. He framed us with both the cops and the bodyguards, hoping we'd get caught in the crossfire. He bolted out the front door as soon as we went up the stairs—that was the door opening and closing I heard—and he's probably a mile away by now.

I hear scuffles down the hall and maybe the guards hear the sirens outside, which grow nearer, louder by the second. Risina and I are going to have a chance, but it's going to be a slim one and we have to do it soon, we have to make our move in those moments of inevitable confusion as the cops make their way on to the scene but don't know exactly what they're rolling into.

I see the bubble lights now, a pair of cruisers, that's it, and they blitz through the gate, knocking it off its hinges, then roar up the driveway, pinning our rental sedan in front of them as both sets of doors fly open and uniformed police officers spill out, guns drawn.

I hear the front door open and one of the bodyguards shouts something and the cops yell back, and that's what I'm looking for . . . a little contact so I can change the pace.

I bust out the bedroom window glass and fire over the cops' heads, BAM, BAM, BAM, into their patrol cars, BAM, BAM, BAM and I hear the front door slam shut and a scared guard scream "he's fucking shooting!" and then the downstairs explodes as the cops retaliate with indiscriminate, panicked firepower.

"Outside! Grab the cigar!" I scream at Risina and she dashes out and back in as quickly as a cat, the cigar held out to me.

I snatch it out of her hand, jam it in my mouth as I collect the sheets off the bed, puff, puff, wadding them up, puff, puff, getting the end of the heater to glow red like a coal in a stove, and then I hold it to the end of the sheets and it doesn't take long, they start to burn, and I toss them to the curtains, which catch fire and go up too as flames curl toward the ceiling and lick the molding.

Confusion is as big a weapon to a professional hit man as a gun, and the more obstacles you can throw at your pursuers the better your chances of survival.

We're out on the patio as the room goes up. We step past K-bomb's dead body and I plant both hands on the railing and hop it, drop from the second story to hit the grass and spring up without tumbling, and I don't have to look back to know Risina does the same.

"Don't shoot a cop unless you have to," is all I have time to say, as we reach the front of the house, and I peek around the corner. The cops are out of their cars, and the two in the near sedan have moved up behind our rental to use it as cover. Smoke starts to pour out of the top floor, and the cops have their firearms pointed at the front door, waiting for the men inside to make a move.

I wait, wait, wait, and then I get the break I expect, the front door opens and one of Kirschenbaum's men shouts, "we're unarmed! We're coming out! No one's firing! It's a goddamn inferno in here!"

"Keep your hands up or we *will* shoot!" shouts back the closest officer, more than a little distress in his voice.

"Don't shoot us, goddammit! We're unarmed! We're coming out! There are four of us!"

And the door swings open wide, as four hacking, wheezing guys make their way out on to the porch, black smoke trailing them. The cops' training kicks in right on cue and all of them bolt for the men. Each grabs a bodyguard and shoves him off the porch and on to the grass out in front as the house really starts to go up, a fireball.

The guys hack up smoke and the cops scream at them to stay the fuck down, to get their hands behind their backs and they pull out their plastic ties to secure the men's hands. It's now or never. I nod at Risina and we bolt for the near cruiser, the one with the engine still idling. Risina ducks for the passenger door, while I hop across the back trunk and swing around to the driver's side.

One of the cops, a young kid with a mop of red hair, must've caught our movement out of the corner of his eye. He swings around, his eyes as wide as plates, and fumbles for his gun.

In a flash, I aim, fire once, and knock him down, and I'm behind the wheel, hitting reverse, gunning the cop sedan out of there, roaring backwards, down the drive and out into the road.

"I thought you said not to shoot a cop!" Risina screams at me from the passenger seat.

"That applied to you, not me."

"Oh man," she starts to say, her hand up on her forehead, so I put a palm on her knee, firm.

"I didn't kill him. I just hit him in the thigh so he wouldn't pop a shot off at us as we fled. He's going to be fine."

She gives me a sideways look to see if I'm fucking with her, but I'm not and I can see relief wash over her like an ocean wave.

We ditch the cruiser three blocks from a shopping center, but not before we wipe it down. The parking lot is full of cars, and I head to the furthest row, where the employees park and won't be out until closing time. I pick a small Honda—the make stolen most often—break in, and crack the ignition. Ten minutes later and we roll out of Ridgefield, headed south on Highway 33.

In the passenger seat, I believe I see Risina smile, but I'm already thinking of ditching this car and finding another one.

# CHAPTER EIGHT

isina and I are in New York, holed up in the St. Regis Hotel on East 55th Street. I have more money than I know what to do with and it might be safer to break my routine and stay somewhere with a little more polish than the usual unkempt inns I frequent when on assignment. Over the years, I collected staggering fees for completing my work. Since the money held no allure for me, I rarely spent any of it; instead, I socked it away in accounts all over the world. My fence kept credit cards up to date for me, and I have safety deposit boxes in over a dozen major cities containing the right plastic and right identities. Holding two of them in my wallet right now reminds me how important it is to find a new fence when this is over if Archie doesn't come out of it alive.

I like New York and its dense population. It's an easy city to get lost in; it's often advantageous to be a needle in a stack of needles.

I need to work out my thoughts. Usually, I'll just talk to myself, but it's nice to have someone to bounce ideas off of. "I think Spilatro put the wheels in motion by kidnapping Archie and then watched them turn. He marked Smoke the whole way, and everything played out how he hoped. I get summoned out of hiding, delivered to his door. He doesn't want to negotiate though, doesn't want to talk, just wants to kill me. Hence the collapsed scaffolding. But that didn't work."

"Then why didn't he pop you with a bullet when we walked through Kirschenbaum's front door? When he could've surprised us?"

"You think I'd've let him? I don't get surprised, Risina. I was prepared for a bodyguard to pull a gun. I just wasn't prepared for that bodyguard to be Spilatro."

She considers that for a moment, then, "But why? Why does he want to kill you? You've never encountered him before. He hasn't been linked to any of your past jobs, has he?"

"I don't know yet. If I had a good fence like Archie, or even a half-decent one like Smoke, at my disposal, he could be gathering information on Spilatro right now to help me figure out the connection between him and me. But I don't."

She runs her hands through her hair, a habit that gives away when she's stumped. She opens her mouth but I interrupt, "There is one thing we have to do now . . ."

"What?"

"In response to a kidnapping, the family usually follows a playbook. They get a ransom note and focus on what the kidnapper wants. They look at the ask and the risks and make a decision whether or not to give the kidnapper his demands, hoping for some sort of break after the exchange, after their loved one is returned safely. But they're looking at it backwards.

"If Archie is still alive—and that's a big 'if' as far as I'm concerned—then giving me up isn't going to get us anywhere. He'll kill me, then kill Archie. There's only one way to take down a kidnapper . . . you have to find something or someone *he* loves and take it from him. Flip the game on his head."

Her eyes track and her head nods as she sees it. "We kidnap something of his right back."

"That's right. Then see if he wants to talk to *us* about making an exchange. Not Archibald Grant for me. Those are his terms, his playbook. We take something or someone Spilatro holds precious and make the exchange about that. We have the leverage. Not him."

"We stay on offense like you said before."

"Exactly. But listen to me, Risina, this is going to get worse, much worse. It's going to get brutal, it's going to get ugly, and we're probably going to have to spill some blood in order to get Archie back. If Archie's already dead, we're going to destroy whomever or whatever Spilatro holds close to him, and then we're going to have to kill him."

She swallows, but nods, then nods a second time as though to reinforce her acceptance. "Remember that he brought us into this, he struck us first, and whatever we have to do is because of him. We didn't ask for this but we're damn sure going to end it. Messages are written in blood in this business."

"A tiger is a tiger."

"That's right. And he should have left me, should have left *us*, sleeping in the jungle."

I go back to that final file, the fourth hit, that had Spilatro working a tandem with the woman named Carla, the same woman Archie then used later for his personal contract. When professional killers work a tandem sweep, when they're working together to accomplish a single hit, it usually indicates a certain closeness. The killers either came up together, or partnered for convenience purposes, or split the fees because they each had a specialty or strength that was necessary for the most effective hit. Rarely are they complete strangers. A degree of trust has to exist in order to execute an effective tandem.

Since all I have on Spilatro is his face, I'm going to need whatever information off of Carla I can get. I struck out with Kirschenbaum, so she's going to have to do.

She won't be on the lookout for me unless they're still tight, which I doubt based on those last three files, the hits Spilatro worked alone, plus the one she worked solo. They went their separate ways, and maybe the reason behind it will help me build a strategy for taking on the son-of-a-bitch who came after me.

Finding Carla is going to require calling in a favor. Looking at the clock, I'm going to have to wake up a fence in Belgium.

A shell game of pre-paid phones and intermediaries and appointment times and coded messages finally lands me a secure connection with Doriot, a Brussels-based fence I've crossed paths with a couple of times in Europe. Once when I went to his office so he could evaluate me, and a second time when I reached him in a prison in Lantin, where he thought he was safely hidden.

"Hello, Columbus. I heard you were dead, so this is a surprise." His thick French accent sounds even rougher over the phone line.

"Still breathing."

"Yes, I can hear that now."

"And you're out of jail."

"I couldn't afford to stay in."

"And how's Brueggemann?"

"Unemployed, I'm afraid."

Brueggemann was a German heavy who helped me find Doriot in that Lantin jail, against his will. I think I exposed his weakness as an employee.

"So you would not be calling me for any reason I can understand unless you need something from me, yes? So how may I help you?"

Belgians tend to get right to the point, a national trait I admire.

"I need you to do something for me."

"I see. What is that something?"

"I need you to locate a New York female hitter who goes by Carla. I need you to hire her for a dummy job. Tell her she has to meet the fence and give her a fake address on Warren Street in Tribeca. I'll pick her up from there."

"You going to put her down?"

"Nothing like that."

"Who's her contracting fence?"

"I'm guessing Kirschenbaum, but he's dead so you'll have to figure out how to contact her."

"I see."

This is the part where he realizes he has me over a barrel and will ask for something. Either money or a favor or to pull a job for him for free. But Doriot is full of surprises.

"Okay, Columbus, how can I contact you?"

I give him the number on a prepaid phone and tell him to text me there with a secure number and then I'll call him back from a different line.

"Very well. I'll try to dial you in the next day or two."

I decide to flush the quail if he's not going to attempt it. "And what do you want in exchange?"

"Not a thing. I have a new outlook on life. I am trying to be accommodating to my friends and rely on providence to reward me with good fortune."

"Uh-huh."

"You are a cynic then. I understand. But my actions will turn you into a believer."

"Okay . . . well, I'll talk to you soon."

"Yes, soon."

We hang up. If he's going to work out his personal issues on my behalf, I'm happy to accommodate.

Carla is in her late thirties, and looks the opposite of most female plugs I've encountered over the years. Professionals are always trying to get close to their marks in order to make the kill in private and get the hell away after business is done; as such, most of the women I've seen in this line of work are gorgeous. They work their way inside on the mark through suggestions of sex and pounce when the target is at his most vulnerable. By the time the mark figures out he's been conned, his bodyguards are outside the door, his pants are around his ankles, and his day is about to be ruined. Many a target has been popped at night, but not discovered until the next morning, naked, in bed, blood-dry.

Carla isn't talking too many men into the bedroom. She's dressed like she's used to towing around a couple of kids: knock-off designer jeans and an unflattering print shirt bearing a vague pattern of stripes. She's dowdy, about thirty pounds overweight, and has a face that wouldn't launch any ships out of Troy.

I smile when I spot her. She wouldn't stand out in any room, on any block, in any crowd, on any stage. She doesn't just blend into the background, she *is* the background. I almost didn't pick her out, even though she's the only woman walking down Warren Street at this time of morning. Her expression is neutral, as bland as her wardrobe and as unassuming as her gait. I like her already.

I approach Carla from behind so she'll have to turn. I want to see how she moves, see if I can spot where she keeps her weapons.

"Carla?"

She turns slowly, deliberately. Her eyes fix on my chest, unchallenging. Her voice is wheezy, like a trumpet with a faulty valve. Nothing about her is inviting.

"You Walker?"

"That's right. Let's move where we can talk."

"You got an office around here?"

"I like to walk and talk."

"You got muscle?"

"Just me."

"You must be new to this."

"I . . . how long I've been doing this is none of your business."

She doesn't respond, just follows beside me as I head up the street toward the river. I think she's bought my newbie act, though I'm not certain.

I talk just above a whisper, "You work tandem with a hitter named Spilatro?"

"Why's it matter?"

"I might need a two-fer and my client wants a team who've worked well together in the past."

"Fsssh." The trumpet hits another false note as she blows out a disappointed breath. "I don't team anymore."

"You guys have a falling-out?"

"Why's it matter?" she asks a second time.

"Just making conversation."

"Now I know you haven't been doing this long."

She stops in the street and this time lifts her eyes all the way to my face. "You got a job? Give me a file and let me know when you want the account closed. Otherwise I'm going to walk in that direction, you're going to walk in that direction, and if we see each other again, we won't be shaking hands."

During this, her face doesn't pinch or blacken. She just says it plainly, like we're discussing the Tribeca weather.

"All right, don't tighten up. I was just trying to get a feel for your style . . ."

"What you see is what you get," she says.

"Fair enough. Let's stop right here."

She obeys and folds her arms, impatient. I change tactics, hardening.

"We're going to have a conversation about Spilatro and you're going to tell me everything you know about him, or you'll be dead at my feet before you can take a step away. Your choice."

This ambush catches her flush, off-guard. She blinks and swallows, not sure how control could have flipped so quickly.

Then her right eye flutters as a red laser shines into it, and we watch together as a small pinprick of red light slowly moves down her face until it stops square in the middle of her chest. Risina is high up on a rooftop working our own loose version of a tandem. Carla doesn't need to know that the red laser comes from an office pointer rather than a gunsight.

I hold my hand up. "If I raise a finger, you drop. Nod if you understand."

It takes her a moment to focus on me, and when she does, it is through defeated eyes. She nods. Her gaze flits back to the red dot on her chest.

"Who are you?"

"What's it matter?" I say, using her words. "What do you know about Spilatro?"

"He . . ."

"Speak up."

"He brought me into this business."

"Oh yeah?"

"Yeah. I . . . uh . . ." She shakes her head slowly, like she can't believe what she's about to say. "I was married to him."

That's unexpected.

"Start from the beginning."

It doesn't take long for the words to gush out of her like water from an overturned hydrant. I have the feeling Carla has been waiting a long time to tell her story, to get things off her chest. Most likely, she hasn't had anyone to talk to about what she does for a living. She just needs someone to whom she can confess her sins, both personal and professional, and I'm the first man to ask for it. That's unexpected, too.

For the first six years of their marriage, Carla Fogelman Spilatro had no idea her husband, Douglas, was a professional hit man. She thought he worked sales for a software company that specialized in creating computer programs for brokerages. He talked about programs for tracking stocks, programs for tracking sales, programs for tracking investments, and it all seemed, well, boring. She tuned him out. She didn't care. She worked too, as a speech pathologist for a hospital, assisting stroke patients who could no longer get their mouths around their words. It was stressful and grueling and demanding, and she came home each day exhausted, too tired to listen to her husband talk about quotas and sales leads.

Their marriage was comfortable if not comforting, and she was happy to have the television to herself when her husband went away on frequent business trips. They had no kids, confessing early in their courtship neither cared for children, and she never heard her biological clock tick the way so many other women did. Between her husband's commissions and her speech salary, they established themselves in the upper middle class and had a nice two-story home, the customary accoutrement of couples earning their income.

Her husband had one quirk. Miniatures. He had a basement full of miniatures—airplanes, trains, cars. In fact, he built elaborate cityscapes, with model skyscrapers and model traffic congestion and model construction equipment and sometimes little model pedestrians walking the model streets. She didn't mind him down in the basement, building his tiny worlds; she figured having him home when he was in town was better than having him out at bars or running around the way some husbands did. Besides, she could watch her shows while he was building and painting down there. She never had to fight him for the remote control.

A text changed her life. A simple text from her friend Michelle.

I DIDN'T KNOW DOUGLAS WAS IN CLEVELAND.
HE'S NOT.
OH. SWORE I SAW HIM. HOW R U?

She didn't respond, and when the TV suddenly sprang to life, she realized she'd been sitting there for the full thirty minutes it took TiVo to override the pause. She looked at her hand and realized she had chewed her thumbnail to the quick.

Doug wasn't in Cleveland. He was on a business trip, yes, but he said he was going to New York to see his client. What was the name he had said? Damn, why didn't she listen to him? Smith Barney? Something like that.

She was being silly. Why was her imagination running wild? Why did she watch stupid trash like *Desperate Housewives* and *Young and the Restless*, where every husband was philandering around like it was Roman times? People in real life didn't act like that, right?

She should just call him on his cell and see where he was. He'd probably said Cleveland anyway. Maybe she had mixed it up. Cleveland and New York?

"Hello?"

"Hey, hon, I can't talk right now."

"Are you in a meeting?"

"Walking into one right now. I'll call you when it's over . . ."

"Are you in . . ." But he hung up before she could finish the question.

She got online and found a number for a Smith-Barney branch in Cleveland. There were three so she picked the first one and dialed the main line.

"Morgan Stanley Smith Barney Financial . . ."

"Yes, hello . . . my name is Carla Spilatro . . . I have to . . . is my husband Doug there right now?"

"I'm sorry?"

"Doug Spilatro with Valsoft?"

"Hold one moment."

She waited, chewing that thumbnail down until she tasted blood.

A new voice came on the line. "Hello, this is Matt Chapman, may I help you?"

"Hi, sorry to bother you. My husband works for Valsoft and I think he has a meeting with someone in your, uh, firm. His name is . . ."

"Don't know any Valsoft. You sure you have the right branch?"

Her heart beat harder. "No, I guess I'm not sure."

"Well, we have two other branches in Cleveland. I'll have Melanie come back on and give you the numbers . . ."

"Thank you . . . oh, wait. Mr. Chapman . . . ?"

"Yes?"

"You said you don't know Valsoft? It's my understanding they produce and manage the software you use on your computers?"

"Hmm. I don't think so. We use good ol' Microsoft."

"Do all the branches use Microsoft?"

"I'm ninety-nine percent sure."

She had moved her teeth off the thumb and on to the cuticles on her ring finger. "Okay, sorry to bother you."

"No problem."

She looked up the Valsoft corporate webpage. It wasn't more than a few pages, but there was her husband's name and contact info under the "outside sales" banner. Sure, the number listed was his cell phone, but he worked out of his car most days. The corporate office's main address was listed as Deerfield, Michigan, and she realized she had never been to Michigan, much less Deerfield. There was a main office phone number, so she picked up the phone to call again.

Then she stopped. What was she doing? One little text from her friend saying she'd seen Doug somewhere other than where he said he was—she was certain he had said New York—and she's running around checking on him like he's some sort of dual-life soap opera character. She put the phone down. She'd wait and talk to him when he returned and just ask him where he went and how the meetings went.

She plopped on to the couch but couldn't concentrate, so she ate an entire quart of Ben and Jerry's Cherry Garcia but still couldn't keep her thoughts straight. She flipped channels and all the networks were breaking in on the soaps to talk about a "major accident" in Cleveland. The Cleveland of it caught her eye. Doug might be in Cleveland and there was an accident there too?

She grew up near there, in Shaker Heights, and knew the skyline well. It seemed a section of light rail track above a highway had collapsed and an RTA train hadn't been able to brake in time. It dove over the edge and killed fourteen people. Such a random, odd event. An act of God. One day you're riding a passenger train, maybe worried about making a meeting on time or concerned about the job interview you're headed to or wondering whether or not you're going to have time to pick up a snack on the way home from work and what stops you cold? A piece of track giving way and it's bye-bye to all those plans you made. Incredible.

A news camera in a helicopter was showing the accident under a "LIVE" banner, a bird's-eye view of dozens of emergency vehicles surrounding the aftermath of the crash like moths circling a flame. As the chopper hovered, it settled on a particular angle, that view of God looking down from above on the carnage, and suddenly she felt as though she'd been jolted with electricity. She shot straight up on the couch and overturned her carton of ice cream as she sent the spoon clattering across the wooden floor.

That angle. The precise angle of the news footage. She'd seen that angle before. She'd seen this accident before.

She had gotten off her ass yesterday to do a bit of cleaning, and decided to vacuum the carpet in the basement when she wouldn't be under her husband's feet. The door was locked, which was odd, but she didn't think too much about it. She knew where her husband stored his keys, even if he had never outright told her. She imagined there wasn't a square inch of this house she didn't know intimately, and so had retrieved the key from its hiding place and gone down below so she could surprise Doug with a clean work area when he returned from New York. Or Cleveland.

She realized her tongue had turned to chalk, thinking about yesterday. She rose from the couch and headed to the basement door. Slowly, she descended the stairs as though she were in a dream, each step bringing her a better view of the table where Doug built his miniatures.

From the back, it looked like any of the dozens of skylines he'd built over the years, though this one had a familiarity to it she hadn't noticed yesterday.

She reached the basement floor without realizing it, her eyes fixed on the model city, crafted with such precise detail. Doug had grown into an accomplished designer; how had she not noticed it before? The level of detail. The precision of the streets and buildings. The photographs pulled from the internet and attached to the corkboard on the wall to serve as blueprints for the model.

She kept gliding around the model, following the path she'd taken with the vacuum cleaner, and her jaw dropped as her eyes led her around the cityscape.

The track was there . . . the light rail track. The exact place where the rail had collapsed according to the news footage was also collapsed here, and a miniature train was shown draped over the broken section, mimicking exactly what had happened.

Doug left on Wednesday. The last time he was in this basement was Tuesday night. The accident happened today? It was live, right? Or was she confused? It was all so . . .

She felt her stomach roll over and she bent at the middle, but nothing came out. Her body reacted before her mind could catch up. What the hell was going on? Why did the floor threaten to pull her down? She fought off the urge to collapse, to faint, and raced back up the stairs toward her computer. Maybe the news was old and it was a replay and she was confused. It only took a second to confirm on CNN.com that the accident was "breaking news," that it had happened today.

What the fuck was her husband up to? What the fuck was he involved in?

He came home the next afternoon. The basement door was wide open. If he was surprised about that, if he felt any moment of shame or regret about her discovery, she didn't know. She was waiting for him when he walked down the stairs, standing with the model between them.

"What did you do?" she barked.

"Carla . . ."

"Just tell me what this means!" She pointed at the model, at the collapsed miniature train. He circled around the table toward her, his arms outstretched, and she wanted to be hugged, needed to be hugged, but she wasn't ready to let him touch her yet. She realized tears were streaming down her face and she tried to blink them away. She had barely slept, had pictured this confrontation a million times since yesterday, but the reality never lines up with the way we imagine it. "What did you do to those peop—"

The last word stuck in her throat as his hands closed around her neck. It took her a full five seconds to realize what had happened, was happening. So sure was she that he was coming around to placate her, to comfort her, to soothe her, that she never imagined he'd try to kill her. She flopped backward into the model, his precise model, and she felt a sting of pain as her back smashed through the light rail track and crushed the rest of the miniature train.

He was strong, much stronger than she would've thought. When did he get so strong? She kicked at him but her legs were on the wrong side and she couldn't gain any traction. Her fingers clawed at his hands but the grip was solid and his face, his horribly twisted face started to blur as tears soaked her eyes. She might have a chance for a couple of words, just a couple if she could get his fingers off her throat.

What had the self-defense expert said in that meeting at the hospital back when they had that rapist scare? Forget the neck. Thoughts whizzed around her head at a million miles an hour. Forget your neck and go for the eyes. His eyes.

She didn't think about it anymore, just went hard for his eyes as she grabbed the side of his head and dug in with her thumbnails. The effect was immediate; he flopped backward, never expecting her to fight back, and she sucked in air like a swimmer coming to the surface.

Recovering, he took a step forward and she managed to screech out: "I took pictures!" The words sounded like they had been scratched with sandpaper, but they hit her husband flush and took hold. He stopped in mid-step, his feet rooted to the ground. His eyes darted back and forth as he tried to figure out his next move. Finally, he spoke. The calmness in his voice chilled her.

"Where?"

"Emailed to my hotmail account."

He started to take another step, when her words stopped him again. "Where do you think the police are going to look when I go missing? You don't know the password to that account, but all my friends have sent and received emails from me there. The cops'll figure out how to open it."

His face was flush with anger. "God. Dammit!" he spat, breaking it into two words so he could hammer the second.

"You stay away from me."

"Just calm the fuck down."

"I mean it."

"I know you mean it, Carla. I know." Then he moved over to a chair, sat down heavily, and rubbed his head in his hands. "Just calm down and let me think."

They went to breakfast. It seemed extraordinary at the time, and now even more so as she retold it to me. He told her everything. Everything. She had him by the balls, so he just came out with it. Maybe it had been weighing on his chest and he wanted to talk about it, just like she was doing now. Maybe he didn't know how to broach the subject with her before this tipping point . . . she didn't know. But over bacon and eggs at IHoP, he told her how he'd first gotten into the killing business after his discharge from the army; an infantryman in his unit had been taking contracts for a decade, and remembered Doug as having particular acumen for planning missions. Doug was adept at reading a map and conducting an ambush and presenting an almost geometrical strategy for accomplishing the squad's goals. You need to raid a building? Go find Doug. You need to take out an ammo dump? Go find Doug.

Ten years later, he was married to Carla and making eighty grand a year in middle-management sales when his old friend Decker knocked on the door and walked him through the business. Gave him the basics on fences and hits and kill fees and tandem sweeps and time commitments and hidden money and weapons caches, all one needed to know to become a professional contract killer. It wasn't much different than planning missions in Kabul, truth be told. Said if Doug were interested, then he'd introduce him to a fence and see how they did together. Said if he wasn't, he'd never see Decker again. It was a crossroads moment and the timing was right: Doug was bored out of his mind and looking for some spice.

The first hit was messy and personal and upsetting. Face to face with a guy in an elevator who never saw it coming, but the blood and the matter and the splatter were enough to make Doug gag every time he thought about it. He had seen violence in Iraq, but it was mostly at a distance, and he was never the one actually pulling the trigger.

But he liked the work. By God, he really did. It was like everything he had ever done in his life was designed to make him an effective killer: his love of statistics and science and numbers and percentages—the very things that pushed him into a computer science degree after his service—also helped him execute the perfect hit. He just didn't like the mess. Even when he was choking her hours before, he knew he wouldn't be able to go through with it. He was in the death business, but he didn't like the actual killing.

It was a paradox, but one to which he spent a month devoting his thinking time. Could he be an effective killer, but from a distance like in Iraq, where he wouldn't necessarily need to see the kill? And in doing so, could he create a new niche in the market?

It hit him in a flash, the way the best ideas most often do. Accidents.

The difficult part in executing a hit is getting away after the mark is murdered. So what if there isn't a murder? What if the death is ruled accidental? Would the client be willing to pay— possibly even pay a premium—if the hit appeared as though the mark were the victim of bad luck?

He floated the question to the fence Decker had secured for him. The man looked at Doug like his head had sprouted antenna. So he shut his mouth, took his next assignment, and started planning.

The mark was an Air Force colonel stationed in San Angelo, Texas. Doug didn't know why someone wanted him dead and he honestly didn't care. He just didn't have much sympathy for people—didn't value their lives; if he were being honest, he never did. Most people were assholes or stuck-up or inferior anyway. And no one lived forever, didn't matter who you were. Why should Doug give a shit if some stranger had his ticket punched?

He knew the colonel lived in a ratty one-story home near the base and so he rigged the building to collapse on him while he slept.

The plan worked, the roof fell in directly on top of the mark, and Doug even added a weight set in the attic so the death would be instantaneous. Except it wasn't. The colonel died, yes, but only after two weeks in the hospital in the ICU as doctors fought for his life. Spilatro sweated those two weeks like his own life hung in the balance. Maybe it did.

When he showed up to his fence after the mark finally died, Doug expected to be reprimanded. But Kirschenbaum clapped him on the back and asked him when he'd be ready to go again. It turned out the client was ecstatic with the way it went down, with the way the police and the press declared it to be a sad accident.

Kirschenbaum apologized for not recognizing what Spilatro brought to the table. He understood now the value in Doug's killing style. He'd like to increase his fee. He was seriously impressed with the innovation. He'd like to step up their relationship. Move Doug to the top of his stable.

Doug was pleased with himself. His father had never once complimented him like this. Nobody had.

So that's how he got into it and that's what he did. He hadn't worked in software sales in years. He was a contract killer, one of the most sought-after Silver Bears in the game. He told Carla how much money they really had, how much he had hidden away in cash, where no bank, no taxman, no creditor could get to it.

"But what about collateral damage?" she asked him. What about the other people who die in these accidents? What about the innocents on the train in Cleveland?

He shrugged. "People die in accidents every day," he told her. "I don't care about them and I don't think about them."

Then he put his hands out across the table, palms up, imploring her to hold hands, as if those same hands hadn't been around her throat two hours before.

"I overreacted," he told her. "But it was such a surprise to see you standing there . . . it was like a violation, I guess. I really apologize for that."

"For trying to kill me?" she whispered as she tried her best not to raise her voice.

"That wasn't me. I promise. I was stressed out and off my game. I was seriously in shock. Nobody's ever thought to catch me before and I guess I hadn't prepared for it mentally. I saw you standing down there and an animal part of me took over. But I'm okay now. I see it now."

Inexplicably, she softened and he pounced on it like a cat with a ball of string. "I love you, honey. That's never changed. You mean more to me than anything. You tell me to stop, to get out, to drop this business and leave it in the sewer, then I will. We'll just move away and be done with it."

And she believed him.

We sat on a stoop on Warren Street for hours while Carla laid it out for me. If she forewent details, I grilled her to fill them in. If I thought she was holding back, I turned up the heat. That laser sight on her chest would disappear for a time, then reappear at various intervals, so it stayed omnipresent in her mind. But I couldn't have pried half this information from her if she hadn't wanted to talk, hadn't *needed* to talk. I don't believe most of it, especially the parts where she presents herself in the best possible light. But the kernels of truth are there, and it is those kernels I can make pop.

"And instead of asking him to quit, you joined him?"

"Not at first. God, no. But you're right, I didn't ask him to quit either. The money was insane, and the job kept him busy. I just put my hands over my ears, hear no evil, see no evil, you know?"

"So when did you start working tandem?"

She gazes at her feet and that laser pinpoints her chest. Dark circles have formed around her eyes now, and her face has gone pallid, as if unburdening herself of this story has discarded her soul with it. "I don't know. Years ago. He asked me if I wanted to help him out once and I guess I said yes. He figured he could charge more for two of us. So I ran interference and helped move a mark into place, but I . . . I never had the stomach for it."

"Uh huh."

She doesn't bother looking up to see the doubt in my expression, content to leave half-truths hanging in the ether like wisps of gossamer.

"You've worked at least one job that I know of on your own since you guys split."

"I have bills to pay."

She blows out a long breath.

"Look, you going to let me go now?"

"I need you to tell me where to find your husband."

"Oh . . . that's right. You want to hire him for a tandem."

I don't say anything. She picks at a piece of gravel on the pavement, crushes it into chalk between her thumb and forefinger.

"All you gotta do is give me one piece of information I can use to find him . . ." I point to that laser sight on her chest, "and you'll never see that dot again."

"The truth is . . ." and for this she looks up, clapping her hands together to wash the dust off. "The truth is . . . you're going to have a very hard time finding him."

"Yeah, why's that?"

"Because Doug's dead."

# CHAPTER NINE

Their last assignment together was the one Archie brokered. Did my name come up during that job? Did Archie mention me casually and Spilatro pounced on the name and came up with a plan to lure me out? Why would he want to?

The answer probably lies in the same reason I turned Archie's office into ash. I knew if those files were left behind, vultures would descend on them to pick over the pieces. There is value in those files, the same value Archie told Smoke about in a prison cafeteria. Information. I've pulled a lot of jobs over the years, some extremely prominent, some that changed the political landscape of this country. If someone knew where to find me, he could broker that information to the relatives of my marks who were looking for atonement. Maybe Archie mentioned he worked with me, and maybe Spilatro turned that into a job for himself, sold my name to the highest bidder while he promised he would be the instrument of revenge.

So why did Carla think Doug Spilatro was dead?

When I was a kid at Waxham Juvey in Western Mass, there was a board game we could check out as long as we played it in the library. It was called "Mousetrap," and it involved building an elaborate, Rube Goldbergian machine to catch a mouse. A crank rotated a gear that pushed an elastic lever that kicked over a bucket that sent a marble down a zig-zagging incline that fed into a chute and on and on until the cage fell on the unsuspecting mouse. But over the years, a few of the plastic pieces went missing and the trap wouldn't spring. We used straws and toothpicks and toothpaste caps to fill in the blanks, rigging it so the cage would drop. The mouse didn't know the real pieces weren't there, and it didn't matter as long as the trap sprung.

I think Spilatro has built his own mousetrap. Psychologically, he takes no pleasure in the kill itself; in fact, it repulses him. So he's thrown all of his passion, all of his expertise, into building elaborate killing machines, elaborate mousetraps. With a living, breathing target, the machine has to be able to contract or expand or adapt based on the movement of the prey. He can build miniatures and plan to his heart's content, but at some point toothpicks have to replace plastic pieces.

So the question is: how much has Spilatro been thrown off of his plan to kill me? Was I supposed to die in the construction accident that claimed Smoke? Was I supposed to get caught in the crossfire at Kirschenbaum's house, trapped between the bodyguards and the police? Or am I still scurrying my way through the mousetrap, tripping a rubber band instead of a crank?

And one more thing: Carla referred to Spilatro as a Silver Bear, even though he takes no pleasure in the actual kill. My first fence taught me that to do what I do, to live with what I do, I have to make the connection to my mark so I can sever the connection later. I have to get inside his head, exploit whatever evil I find there, so I can continue to the next job. What I'm missing from all this, what I still don't know, is *why* Spilatro singled me out. What connection do we have?

Carla and I move from the stoop on Warren Street to a coffee shop around the corner. I tell her she doesn't have to worry about getting shot, that I just want to hear the rest of her story, but my words don't seem to lift any weight off her shoulders. She sits like a prisoner in the corner of a cell, with no hope of rescue. I know Risina is out there watching, and I wonder if she can see the effects the killing business has on its participants.

"The last job. The one you did for Archie. Tell me about it."

"Archie?"

"Archibald Grant. He was the fence."

"Oh. Yes, Archie Grant. I only talked to him on the phone."

"You never met him face-to-face?"

"I didn't meet anyone except for K-bomb. And he, I only met once." She holds up one finger. "He came to me after the job you're talking about, when I was still trying to figure out what the hell I was gonna do now that Doug was gone. I never knew the fence's name before that. I didn't even know what a fence was, to tell you the truth. He just showed up and asked me if I wanted to continue working. I'll be honest, I've only pulled a couple of jobs on my own. Today's call came in from a third party and I thought it was weird and my antenna went up, but I showed up anyway because I don't know what the hell I'm doing anymore. Should've known . . ."

"Yeah, well, here you are. If it makes you feel better, I'd've gotten to you one way or another."

She shrugs. "Maybe."

"Tell me about that last tandem job. I want to hear every detail."

"You have to understand, Doug only told me the bare minimum to keep me involved. I was the flash of light, the honking horn, you know what I mean?"

I shake my head.

"The distraction. The feint. The thing that causes the mark to look one way when death is coming from the other direction."

"Bait?"

"Look at me. Do I look like bait?"

"I meant . . ."

"I know what you meant. Sure, I'd meet a few of the marks. Get 'em to a particular spot Doug would designate in the run-up. That was tough for me, I gotta say. It's one thing to see these targets from afar, another to shake their hands, hear them speak, watch 'em smile or what not."

"The last job . . ."

"Yeah, I'm getting there. I'd been off for a while. I know Doug was taking contracts and fulfilling them without me. Two or three in a row and truth be told, I didn't mind. I thought I'd like the adventure of it, the game, you know, but when I was lying in bed each night, I'd think about those men I helped put under, and I had a real hard time closing my eyes."

She's checking my face, looking for a sympathetic nod, but I give her nothing. She blows a bit on the top of her coffee before taking a sip.

"Anyway, he'd been home for a while and I knew he must've gotten a new gig because he spent a lot of time down in the basement. I'm talking a good two months, only coming up for a meal, a smoke, a bathroom break, or bed. I figured he was going to work this one solo, but this particular Sunday, he calls me down there.

"This is a simple one, he tells me. Police detective in Boston who drinks too much. This cop must've tossed the wrong guy in the can, because there's a price on his head and Doug is collecting. The procuring fence wanted it to be a tandem, to make sure it went down on a certain day, and Doug convinced the acquiring fence that he'd supply the other contract killer. Me. So this fence . . ."

"Archie Grant," I interrupt. I keep mentioning his name to see if it'll elicit a response, but so far, nothing.

"If you say so. Anyway, Doug tells me this fence is skeptical, but Doug insists on bringing me on, and we can kill two birds with one rock. We'll work the tandem and we'll make sure it looks like an accident. I guess that satisfied what's-his-name, because Doug got the gig and procured the down payment for both hitters.

"I remember thinking, *so this is why you want me to work with you now . . . so you can collect double fees on the same hit.* Say what you want about Doug, the man knew how to game a system no matter what it was. You thought you were pulling the strings? That's only cause he let you think so. He was the one working the puppets, didn't matter what the play was. It wasn't till I saw him doing it to others that I realized all these years, he'd been doing the same to me, you know? I guess that's neither here nor there now, but there it is.

"So getting back to this hit . . . Doug built this elaborate model of this alleyway in Boston. Painted and sanded and lit up to the very last detail. The bar where this detective liked to drown his sorrows was specially made with a flying roof so he could take it off and you could see inside. It was like nothing you ever saw. This one made the one he did for Cleveland look like a kindergartner's shitty homework assignment. Doug had little bartenders in there, little dishwashers, little beer mugs, even miniature peanut shells on the floor. The works.

"So he starts talking me through the plan. This mark comes in this joint every Saturday night like clockwork and stays not only till the bar closes, but after the owner locks the front door. The target is chummy with the owner or shaking him down or whatever but he gets special treatment, one last glass of whiskey on the house before the lights go out. The owner's a salty old Southey who fixes that last highball himself before running receipts in his office until the mark finally heads out the back door.

"So Doug has this plan. It involves me showing up just as the doors close, pretending to be a health inspector. I'm supposed to do a few hocus pocus maneuvers, you know, get the front door locked, slip a roofie in the mark's drink, keep the owner occupied in his office or the kitchen, wave our target out the back door, and that's just half of it. Doug's showing me this elaborate set up he's got worked out in the alley, real domino rally type stuff, ice on the steps, trip wire on the bottom, a lever that'll whack his feet out from under him so that he'll nail the back of his head on the ice, five other things I'm forgetting about. Complicated stuff and his eyes light up as he's telling me all about it.

"I tell him it's all too complicated and for just a moment, he looks at me the way he did when I confronted him in the basement when I first found the model. Oooh, boy, if the devil wears a face, that's what it looks like. I shut up quick and he catches himself like he stepped past the caution signs and straightens up right away but it was there and I saw it. He smiles and tells me how hard he's worked and how even if it's a small job getting a drunk to slip on some icy steps, he wants it done right. He's made a career out of getting it done right and I know better than to pop off again, so I button it and say however he wants to plug this guy is fine with me. I did not want to see that look again, I can assure you that.

"The night of the hit, everything is fine. I'm with Doug running lookout while he sets up the pieces of the trap in the alley.

I haven't seen him work like this and I can tell he's excited about it, the way he's moving around, a smile on his face, all hopped up like a football player before a big game, you know? Like a kid on Christmas Eve? He's wearing a BWSC uniform— Boston Water and Sewer—and a fake beard and all that seemed *unnecessary* looking back but it made him happy so what the hell was I gonna say? He signals me when the trap is all set, and right on time, I hit the front door, just as the owner is cleaning up. Health Inspector is the best cover you can use with bars or restaurants because no one questions it—the manager or owner is mildly annoyed but always accommodating. This was no different and I got the mickey into the detective's drink while the owner and he looked up at a fire exit with a faulty light I pointed out. No big deal. It's amazing how many things people miss each day when they're made to look in a certain direction, you know? Look at the birdie over there while I take the wallet from your back pocket here. People, for the most part, are suckers.

"The plan goes exactly the way Doug drew it up. I took the owner to his office while he told the cop to head out back. I watched out of the corner of my eye, you know, as our target got up and stumbled off. I counted to a hundred in my mind, all while I was talking about grease traps and proper temperatures on the refrigeration system and where the 'wash your hands' signs have to be displayed in the bathroom and I could see the owner's eyes glaze over.

"Abruptly, I get to a hundred and I tell him everything looks good and he can count on a top notch report and can he let me out the front? Doug had told me the probabilities were he would follow me out since he liked to park his Dodge Charger right out in front of his bar. Sure enough, he comes with me outside and I watch from across the street as he climbs into the muscle car and drives away."

"So where's the complication?"

"There wasn't one, is what I'm saying. Not on this job . . ."

"So . . ."

"So I go to meet Doug at the rendezvous spot which is three blocks away, this street corner near a motel and he's got this smile big as summer on his face, you know? I'll never forget it. He's really happy. Says it went off without a hitch. Drunk detective stumbles down the stairs, the lever sweeps his feet, he cracks his skull, out cold. No way he won't freeze to death. Doug even rigged it so some water would spill off the gutter above him, ensuring the detective would be found as frozen as a popsicle. No other way to rule this one but straight up accidental death."

"What about the lever?"

"Doug fixed it with a string so he could slide it away. Everything planned to the last detail, like I said. This is how his mind worked.

"He told me all about the kill as we walked toward the car. I remember thinking I hadn't seen him this happy since before we were married. And I was happy too, as weird as that sounds. I started seeing this life together, this future together. Me and Doug, a team. Other couples can sit on their asses watching the evening news while we'll be out—I don't know—changing the world. That's something you do, you know? You imagine the work you're doing is for the greater good although it's probably just settling some small-time scores. Maybe we can make this work, I thought. Maybe this partnership is all we need to make it work between us, better than it ever was before. It seems silly now, but that's what was going through my head.

All of a sudden, this black van roars around the corner and I get the uneasy feeling it's coming up on us. You know that feeling? The kind that warms you up even though it's cold as balls outside? Doug puts his arm around me all protective like and I remember thinking that was kind of a sweet touch, you know? He wasn't much of an affectionate person, but he thought to put his arm on my shoulders and I thought that was nice.

"The van barrels up and skids to a stop and three sort of gangster looking guys get out, one black and two white and they call Doug by name. 'You Spilatro?' the biggest one says. Doug doesn't answer, but I can hear his breathing stop and truth be told, I was scared to death. I hear another guy say, 'yeah, he's Spilatro,' and I see this guy's face as he steps into the light and he's looking a little familiar, like maybe I know him from somewhere, and I'll be damned if it isn't Decker, his old army buddy, the one who brought him into the killing life. After Doug told me about him, I looked him up in some of Doug's old army pictures, and this is the same guy, I'm sure of it. Doug realizes it at the same time as me and I can see him sigh heavily, like this is all just too much. The first guy, the muscle, raises his hand up and he's holding a gun, some kind of big automatic. Don't ask me what kind because I don't know. The last thing Doug says is 'don't kill my wife,' and crack, crack, the muscle shoots him twice in the chest. Blood flies on to me, I feel it hit the side of my face, and out of the corner of my eye I see Doug drop straight down. You know what I mean? Straight down like all his muscles shut down at once? Well, I just stood there like a jackass, you know, and the three guys pick up Doug's body and throw it in the van. Decker turns and looks at me and I think maybe he's deciding whether or not to drop me too, but he just gives me that hard stare men are so fond of, moves around to the driver's side, and varoom, they're gone. If this was retaliation for something Doug did, nobody said and I don't know. The van drove off as though nothing ever happened and I stood there, I swear for an hour or two, not in shock but not thinking either, you know?"

Her voice falls quiet and she takes a sip of her coffee, not raising her eyes. She doesn't have to blow on it this time.

I give her a moment to play it out, check to see if she's going to say more, and I have to give her an ounce of respect. She doesn't try to conjure up a tear or manage a sob.

I lean back and wait. Everything I do, every interaction hinges on the principle of dominance. Dominance can be physical, like cracking a man in the knee to drop him in front of you so he knows you're better than he is. Or it can be mental: a game of wits, a look, a gesture, a word—anything to gain an advantage over an adversary. Sometimes dominance can simply mean waiting.

After a couple of silent minutes, she looks up, eyes dry. There's resentment in her eyes, resentment for making her draw this out. Finally, when I have her broken, I speak up.

"You know he's not dead."

"You want me to say it?"

"Why pretend?"

She moves the coffee cup back and forth in front of her, grimacing. "He didn't have to do it for me. He could've just walked."

"Didn't have to hire the guys, you mean."

"Yeah. Plan the whole thing out. Tack it on to the end of the other job, you know?" She stops looking at me, at the inside of the diner, at anything. "It was actually . . . well, it was the sweetest thing he did for me the whole time we were married."

I nod, but this is not good. Not good at all.

"Can I get out of here now? I'm done with this."

She's drained now, played out, bitter. If I squeeze her any more, she'll pop.

I nod and she hauls herself up, then hovers over me for a second as her shadow falls across half my face. "It's a bad thing you've done, making me say it." I don't look at her. "It's a bad thing you've done." When I feel the shadow move away, I know she's gone.

We meet in a pre-determined spot, a bench in Battery Park. It's quiet here this time of day. A patch of green. The water. An old man sits at a table by himself, moving chess pieces around while his lips move. Risina is already sitting when I arrive. For a moment, we don't speak. Anyone passing would think us two office drones meeting for a quiet date; the guy in sales with the girl from accounting.

"You let her leave."

"Yeah. She was used up."

I put my arm around Risina, and she leans into me. For just a few short breaths, we're back in that fishing village halfway around the world. Maybe this is all we'll have for a while.

"I thought the idea was to kidnap someone he loves . . ."

"It is. But he doesn't love her."

"He didn't have to set it up for her like that. He could've run off."

"That's true."

"So that means something."

"He loves the process, not her. He loves the mousetrap. He loves setting up all the pieces and knocking them down. He cooked up the dummy fall at the same time as he plotted out the actual kill. Brought her in on the tandem and made the whole thing one piece, you see? First the kill, then the fall . . . two parts of the same job. In his mind, they were always one. He doesn't care about her . . . he gets off on the complication."

Risina frowns. "But he thought to do it that way. It has to be a sign of . . . well, at least affection if not love."

"Maybe. But it's not enough for what we need."

She starts to speak, but I get there first. "When I first understood which way this was breaking, I thought maybe I could enlist Carla to help us find Spilatro and hurt him. The way he treated her, faking his death, bringing this world into her life and then walking away? He left her holding the bag. I thought maybe she was bitter and we could use that bitterness. But she's not. And she's not the opposite either. She's not accepting. She's just . . . finished."

Risina nods. The old man stands and collects his pieces. His lips move, but his words are lost in the wind.

"So we still have nothing. After all this?"

"I didn't say that. She gave us a great deal more than we had before we found her. We know Spilatro was married, we know he was in the army, we know he worked in software sales, at least for a while. We have ways to find him."

"And we know how he thinks."

I smile. Risina's intuition continues to surprise me. "That's right. Now we know how he thinks."

We're going to get to him through his friend, the army buddy who brought him into the game. I notice I'm thinking in plural pronouns again, "we" instead of "I," and I like the way it sounds in my head. The tandem didn't work for Doug and Carla, but they're not us, not even close to us, and Carla served only as a convenience to him. He was using her for cover, that's it. That was her utility for him.

We're not like them at all. Carla said she saw a future for them in the moments before that future was wiped away, but he was the one who caused that plan to fail. It's different for Risina and me. We can pull jobs together, back each other's play, watch each other's back. I fell in love with Risina because of the animal inside her, just below the surface. She has more sand than I imagined back in Rome. She demonstrates it over and over. It's like I'm waiting for the other shoe to drop, even though she's not wearing any. We're not like them. We. Not I. We.

A tiny piece of information can be like a keyword to unravel a code. Based on Carla's story, I know approximately how old Spilatro is, and I know his army buddy's name, Decker, and I can guess a pretty accurate timeline of when they must have been in the service together. From there, it's a reasonable amount of digging to cross-reference the two names, and if the names are false, as I'm sure they will be, then it's a bit more cumbersome but not unconquerable to find similar names who served in the same unit. Most hit men aren't too creative in coming up with their aliases.

This is fence work, but most of the fences I know seem to be missing or dead. About that, K-bomb was right. I do have bad luck with fences.

Still, there is one I know who can be of service and is alive and free: the one in Belgium who has a new appreciation for handing out favors.

Doriot meets us two days later in a barbershop in the basement of the St. Regis. A pair of brothers own the joint, having taken over from their father, good guys, and when I reached out to them to use their place for an after-hours meeting, alone, they didn't hesitate to give me a key. A thousand-dollar tip on a shave and a trim didn't hurt to solidify the deal.

"I told you providence would smile on me for treating you respectfully, Columbus, and here I am in New York City, the Big Apple, so what can I do for you and how much can I be expected to earn? Not that I am only in it for the money since I like you so much, but business is business as I'm sure you understand."

"I need a file on a guy."

"Twenty thousand," he says immediately.

"Give me a fucking break. Twenty thousand . . ."

"I have a ten percent relationship with my hitters, Columbus. This is what I make . . ."

"Bullshit."

"Okay, fifteen . . ."

I could press him to twelve but I don't want to hurt his feelings before he goes to work for me. I'd rather cough up a few extra grand than have to worry about his effort.

"Fifteen's a deal but I don't want to decide on a play from your file and then find out the information is lacking."

He shakes his head vigorously, feigning offense. "I do this right for you, you maybe come back to me for more work. I see how this goes. You'll have a file so filled with truth you can lay it on top of the Bible."

"All right then."

"So who must I find for you?"

I give him everything I know about Decker and Spilatro as I regurgitate my conversation with Carla.

"How much time do I have?" he asks when I'm done.

"Three weeks enough?"

He frowns as though he's thinking about it. "Are you sure you can't come up to eighteen?"

"Fifteen."

"Okay, okay. I'm just asking the question. I'll start right away. You'll see. You have never worked with a fence like me. This file will be like Brussels chocolate." He does that chef thing of kissing the tips of his fingers.

"I need one other thing."

He pauses at the door, then surveys the barber implements surrounding us. "If you tell me you need me to trim your hair, then I'm afraid you will have to come up with the twenty thousand after all." He produces a short laugh that sounds more like a smoker's cough.

"I need to rent a house upstate until your file is ready. Somewhere in the country, somewhere back from a road, somewhere no one's gonna visit, even a mailman. Leave a key and an address for Jack Walker at reception tomorrow and you can have your twenty."

He smacks his lips and raises his eyebrows.

"You sure you don't want a haircut too?"

"Just the keys."

He smiles and heads out the door.

I want to see her kill something.

The house is a good find, a fifteen-minute drive inside the property line from a dirt road only marked by an unassuming gate. I walked the fence line on our first few days and it's over five miles from front to back and side to side. Doriot suspended mail service while we're renting the place, and I have yet to hear a car engine anywhere in the vicinity.

The woods surrounding the house are as thick as a blanket and teem with life. Deer, badgers, squirrels, woodchucks, robins, sparrows and quail go about their days foraging and fighting. I need to see her kill something. I don't care about the hunt or her ability to keep silent or her ability to hold the gun steady or her nerve in pulling the trigger. It's the *after* I'm worried about, the *after* I need to see. How she reacts to blood spilled by her own hand. Will she be like Spilatro and shy away from the mess? Or will she be like me and seek out another opportunity? And which do I really want?

"Why do you carry a Glock?"

"It's a good, lightweight semi-automatic that'll hold seventeen bullets in the clip and one in the chamber. It's made of polymer so it doesn't warp in bad weather and it takes just a second to slam in another clip if you're in a spot."

She smirks and racks a round into the chamber. Her eyes narrow in a mock display of gravity, like she's playing a character in an action film, and then she laughs.

"You still think this is fun and games?"

"I think you need to break the tension sometimes or this would all be overwhelming."

"Sometimes you have to rely on that tension, use it to heighten your senses."

"Or break it to relax."

"Who is teaching whom here?"

"Oh, come on. Don't look at me like that. You want me to say I'm scared, I'll say it without shame. I've been scared since the moment you came back from the bookstore with that look on your face. I haven't stopped being scared. If I paused to think about it, I'd probably start screaming and I don't know that I'd be able to stop. But I've always been good at learning and I've learned by watching you. I keep the fear inside and I make jokes and I laugh and I talk back and I try to look cool and all of that is to keep the fear choked down. So let me do this my way, please. I don't ask much of you and I pay attention, but you have to let me do this my way."

I move in and pull her into me and we stand in the forest as the world falls silent. I'm not sure if I'm holding her or she's holding me, and when we break, her eyes are wet.

"Can you at least make the jokes better?"

She starts to react, then realizes I'm having fun with her. "You shouldn't do that when I have a pistol in my hand."

"You haven't even taken the safety off."

She looks down at the grip and when she does I snatch the gun from her hand.

"Oldest trick in the book."

She starts laughing, hard. The woods come to life again.

A squirrel darts into the path in front of us. It's a bit wary and cocks its head to the side to give us a once-over. It sniffs the air, hops twice more across the path, and rears on its hind legs again to gauge whether or not we present a threat.

Risina stops, levels her gun, and before I can say anything, she pulls the trigger, once, twice, three times, missing the first two shots low before she corrects and sends the creature pinwheeling backward, tumbling end over end like a bowling pin, its hide a mess of blood and fur.

"Anything else you want me to kill?" she asks, unsmiling.

I study her face, and she breaks eye contact to saunter off. I'm starting to think I don't need to worry about the after. Maybe, instead, I should be worrying about what I've created.

He's waiting for us in the cabin.

That fucking bastard Doriot must've sold us out, and I never saw it coming. Didn't even have an inkling it was coming. I've grown too fucking seat-of-the-pants on this whole mission . . . except it's not really a mission, is it? Christ, I should be shot in the head. Ever since I brought Risina into this and I didn't have a fence and I thought I could call in favors and I thought the name Columbus still meant something, it has been one thing after another and I still haven't learned. And that's the rubber meeting the road right there. Columbus. The name carries no weight. Not anymore.

When I was incarcerated in Waxham, I learned a term called "chin-checking." Roughly translated, it describes a gang leader who returns to his neighborhood after time in the joint. While he was gone, some young buck stepped in to fill his shoes in the power vacuum. The ex-con has to reassert his authority by walking up and punching the new kid right in the fucking mouth. Chin-checking. Hello, I'm back. I thought stepping back into this life would be like I never left, except I did leave, and memories are short. Doriot used to be afraid of me, but he's not anymore. If I get through this, Doriot's gonna learn a new term.

I open the cabin door and a cell phone is standing up on the table like a scar. Risina senses something is wrong the way animals perk up whenever a predator roams nearby. The phone rings before I can say anything to comfort her.

If he wanted to kill us, he could've shot us when we walked inside the door. If he wanted to plant a bomb in the phone, then we're already dead. But in my experience, people call when they want to talk.

Risina shakes her head but I press the green button on the phone.

"Hello."

"You've been asking about me."

"You wanted to flush me, here I am."

"You presume to know my intentions?"

"I know a few things. I'll learn more."

"I'll help you out. Here's a fact about me: I'm smarter than you."

"That why you missed me outside the restaurant in Chicago?"

"Who says I missed?"

"It was sloppy."

"Accidents are sloppy by nature. And sloppy by design."

"And the police at Kirschenbaum's house?"

"Now looking for a murderer who happens to fit your description."

"Not exactly the way you drew it up."

He chuckles, and the sound is disturbing in its confidence. "You don't sound sure about that."

He's right. I don't. Even this conversation feels like I'm being spun whichever direction he wants me to go.

"You want—"

But I cut him off in a clumsy attempt to gain control. "What's your play?"

"I don't—"

"Why kidnap Archie Grant? Why call me out by name?"

"You gonna let me finish?"

Is this how boxers feel as a round slips away? Right hooks coming but you're just too slow or tired or old or rusty to get out of the way?

"Is he alive?"

"Check the phone."

The phone beeps in my hand, an incoming text message. I click on it without hanging up the line and there is a picture of Archie holding a *New York Times* with a photograph of a blazing inferno on the front page—fire trucks out and about, spraying the flames down, and I have no doubt if I drive to a newsstand, it'll be today's paper. Archie looks defiant in the photo, a *fuck you* face if I ever saw one. I put the phone to my ear again.

"Satisfied?"

"Let me talk to him."

"He doesn't feel like talking."

"What's this about? Why the games? You want me, here I am."

"You contact my wife again and I'll blow Mr. Grant up in front of you. You'll walk around a corner or step off an elevator and he'll be tied up sitting in a chair. You'll barely have time to register what is happening before parts of your friend slap you in the face."

"Come on. You wanted to flush me? You flushed me. Let's finish this out in the open." Flailing. Too tired. Stumbling.

"You'll be out in the open, Columbus. You won't know where I'll be."

"Just tell me what this is about. I don't mind spinning in circles, but at least tell me why I'm spinning."

And right when I don't think he's going to say anything else, he surprises me. "Dark men."

I've heard that expression once before, in a hotel room in the Standard Hotel in Los Angeles, from the lips of the Speaker of the House of Representatives, the Democratic Nominee for President, Abe Mann, moments before I killed him. *"When I had my problem with your mother, some dark men made that problem disappear. You understand about dark men, I take it . . ."* he had said.

He went on to tell me about the men who were the real players behind the politicians, the dark men who moved the representative's mouths like ventriloquists, the dark men who wouldn't let their candidates, candidates like Abe Mann, leave the game. So the Speaker of the House hired a killer named Columbus and designated himself as the target. His only escape was death, and I was his suicide method.

The dark men must not have been happy about that decision. All this time I was worried about someone in law enforcement tracking me down, but now I see my anxiety was misplaced. I killed the man I was hired to kill, but I upset the dark men who wanted him alive so they could keep pulling his strings. It seems they've held his death against me all these years and now they've hired Spilatro to exact their revenge. He went to them with my name and they said "bring us his head." This changes everything.

Risina and I leave the house immediately, and instead of planning our next move, I just drive. The sun is heading west, dropping toward the horizon, so fuck it, I drive into it headlong, the light fierce in my eyes but maybe that's the way it's supposed to be. Maybe I deserve it. Maybe I've stuck to the shadows for too long and need to spend a little time with the sun in my eyes. Maybe some light will clean my fucking head.

Risina is pensive as she fights the urge to speak. Farms roll past the window, looking properly pastoral. After a moment, she pivots toward me. "What did he mean by dark men?"

"An old job. I probably upset a few apple carts."

"So these men want revenge?"

"Yes."

"And they hired Spilatro to kill you?"

"I think so."

She nods. "Why him?"

"I think he went to them with my name."

"You think Archie gave you up?"

I chew on the inside of my lower lip, and a new idea takes shape in my head.

"I don't believe so . . . I think there's a second explanation."

"Give it to me."

"What if these dark men work for the government? The CIA?"

"And . . ."

"And Spilatro was a soldier."

"So?"

"So . . . what if he never left the military?"

We pull into a Hampton Inn somewhere outside the Berkshires. I switch cars at a used car lot, paying too much but not enough for the salesman to remember us. I choose a room at the inn on the first floor, in a corner with two windows and an outside door nearby in case we need to split in a hurry. I may not be all the way where I was three years ago, but I'm starting to take the smoothness off the edges.

After we make some bad coffee in the four-cup maker provided by the inn, Risina and I take a moment to sit and rest and think.

"You have that look in your eye."

"What do you mean?"

"That same look you gave me that last day in our house before we headed to the US. You look like you want me to leave."

"We're entering new territory here. I've spent my professional life in a world I understand. A world of outlaws. Government agents are a separate entity entirely. They have resources I don't have, access I can't imagine. We have to work around the law . . . they break laws with impunity."

"It doesn't matter. We're in this together until the end. Spilatro knows about me. He's probably known about me since we landed in Chicago."

I nod. She's right.

"If you tried to take care of this on your own, he'd find me and use me against you. There's no sending me away. No hiding me somewhere. If you're not watching me, then you won't know I'm safe. And he'll compromise you at a point when it'll matter."

I keep nodding.

"I love you. I'll do whatever you tell me at this point. If you tell me to run, I'll run. If you tell me to hide, I'll do it. I'll wait for you to come back to me. But it's not the smart play, as you call it. He knows about me, and he knows you love me."

"I do."

"You'll just have to be your best with me dragging on your back."

"No."

Her eyes flash. "What is this 'no'?"

"No, I won't drag you on my back. You're going to have to step up and be the tiger I know you have inside you."

She sets her jaw, and when she looks up, her eyes fill with resolve. "I can be a tiger."

"You're going to have to kill more than a squirrel."

"I will pull the trigger when I have to."

"Then let's find Lieutenant Decker."

# CHAPTER TEN

**W**e backtracked through the four files we had on Spilatro, the four hits Archie assigned. And there it was. The connections between all those jobs that Risina and I and Archie himself had failed to catch. The first hit, the rich female English professor at Ohio State, had helped finance a PAC set up to block government land use for military training in Ohio. For the second, the TV reporter had been working on a story about bribes involving the top senator from Illinois. The unlucky bookkeeper in the third file had more than a few Washington clients on his ledgers. And the final file? The police detective in Boston? The one Carla helped knock over? He would've testified against two NSA officials who were caught with hookers and cocaine at the Intercontinental in downtown Boston if he hadn't slipped on the ice and had such an untimely accident. All Spilatro kills . . . all with government ties. And the fact that all those deaths looked like accidents was the icing on the cake. If they had looked like actual hits, actual assassinations, there would have been inquiries, scandal, attention paid. The dark men wanted these issues to disappear, not become headlines. Spilatro's killing style was perfect for these kinds of jobs.

I wonder if Archie knew he was a patsy for the government, and to what degree he was playing ball. I wonder if he slipped and accidentally gave Spilatro my name, or Spilatro discovered it and then sought out Archie, worked his way inside. Used Kirschenbaum to make himself available to Archie, then worked a few government jobs for him to gain trust. I wonder how extensive the Agency is involved in the private killing business and how many of my assignments over the years were actually financed by taxpayers.

Finally, I look up the light rail accident in Cleveland, the one Carla claims to have discovered in her basement, the one where a section of the rail collapsed, killing the 14 passengers on board. Sure enough, three of the passengers worked for a top Defense contractor, McKnight International. Why the government wanted them dead, and what contract that helped to close, I have no idea.

But Spilatro works for Uncle Sam and has been all along, I'm now sure of it.

It takes her a week in DC. I remain uncertain on whether or not she's capable of shooting a man in the head, but as a researcher, she's extraordinary. This is an Ivy League-educated woman who built an impressive rare book collection by carefully researching titles, cross-referencing sources, compiling lists of potential dealers, wooing and cajoling and nudging reluctant sellers while she gathered the best information first, so she could swoop in and procure a title before her competition knew there was a deal to be made. My mistake, I'm beginning to realize, was grooming Risina to do what I do, to be a contract killer. I've been working with a natural fence the whole time.

She won't need to blend in, to hide in plain sight; in fact, she can use her beauty to secure what she needs, to make men *want* to help her. She can use an arrow I don't have in my quiver: she can be wholly unthreatening.

She made an appointment with the Assistant Secretary of Defense for Public Affairs at the Pentagon, posing as a freelance journalist. With the Presidential initiative for a more transparent government coupled with the Freedom of Information Act and countless journalistic precedents, it wasn't difficult for Risina to gain access to enlistment records. She charmed the ASOD as she explained she was writing a heartwarming article on Desert Storm veterans who had parlayed their time in the service into high-end jobs. So much of what is reported in the mainstream media focuses on the negative, she told him—the combat fatigue, the stress disorders, the disabilities—she was hoping to chronicle the positive effects on veterans who served their country well and made something of their lives after their tour of duty, using the skills they learned in the military to achieve civilian success. The assistant secretary damn near threw his spine out of alignment bending over backward to help her.

Roland Deckman, aka "Decker," and Aaron Spittrow, aka "Spilatro," both joined the army in 1988. Like I said, most hit men aren't too imaginative when they come up with their killing names, and Risina made short work of spotting two similar names in the same unit. They entered the 24th ID out of Fort Stewart, Georgia, one of the first units deployed to Saudi Arabia in the summer of 1990. When the Gulf War began, the 24th faced some of the fiercest resistance in the entire campaign, running up against the 6th Mechanized Division of the Iraqi Republican Guard. They still managed to capture the airfields at Jabbah and Tallil. Deckman and Spittrow worked as infantry grunts, nothing unusual in their service records.

The ASOD apologized to Risina profusely, but contact information on Deckman and Spittrow was sketchy following their military service. They both were honorably discharged in 1992, and where most soldiers would at least have a few files of contact and discharge information, those files seemed to be missing for Deckman and Spittrow. Risina asked if there was contact information from *before* they joined the army.

The ASOD smiled. That, he had. At least for one of them.

Northville, Michigan is a quiet slice of suburbia outside of Detroit, with modest homes peppered around mansions. Although many neighborhoods in Detroit look as though they've been abandoned and forgotten, Northville could just as easily be situated outside Kansas City, Chicago, or Dayton. It is filled with regular folks making livings and raising families. Roland Deckman grew up here before he joined the army.

We drove straight to Michigan, taking shifts behind the wheel. Risina spent enough time driving in the States when she was in college that she isn't intimidated by the width of our highways. In fact, she handled our sedan like it was primed for the Indy 500.

"Do you know what the fastest car in the world is?" she asked as we blasted through Ohio.

"What?"

"A rental car."

Well, at least her jokes have gotten better.

It's warm and rainy when we arrive, the kind of summer shower unique to Michigan that blows down like hell for fifteen minutes before it exhausts itself and retreats out to the lake.

We sit outside Deckman's parents' house. He's now a government assassin, I'm sure of it, a breed of animal I've been fortunate to avoid until recently. He's had training I've never had, supplies I can only dream of, access to targets that must be facilitated by entire teams of personnel and equipment, and a get-out-of-jail-free card that removes half the worry of making a kill.

But does he secretly despise his job? Does he question the political motivations behind his assignments? Does he rely too heavily on the system? Do his fortunes change with each new administration? And does this cement his loyalty to his friend Spilatro over his loyalty to his employers?

The real question, the only question that matters: is he a tiger?

No, I haven't had to worry about government hitters until now, until they sought me out, forced me back in when I was content enough to ride out my days in obscurity.

We sip coffee and wait for the rain to die.

"Decker's our key. He's who we're going to trade for Archie and how we're going to get them off me."

"What makes you think Spilatro or Spittrow, or whatever his name is, will be more willing to deal for Decker than Carla?"

"Because these cover stories people tell are mostly lies but always have moments of truth. I think Decker has been Spilatro's friend and fellow soldier for twenty-plus years. I think they were already working jobs together when they were in the service. I think Decker went to the CIA first and rescued Spilatro from a dead-end life of middle-management and that formed a bond that is unbreakable.

"I could be wrong. He could mean nothing to Spilatro. But he helped him pull off that fake hit to fool his wife. After all that time, they were still together. My guess is the Agency isn't too keen on fostering or facilitating friendships . . . they'd want their officers working alone and anonymous. So these guys still pulling a job together has to mean more than blood . . . it has to. At least, that's what I'd like to believe."

"Because it's the best plan?"

"Because it's all we have right now."

The military is one thing, the CIA quite another. She couldn't get inside Langley the way she did the Pentagon, so the only chance we have of confronting Decker has to come from his past. Spilatro certainly covered his tracks, burning down the "Aaron Spittrow" military records from both before and after his service, but Decker must've been comfortable no one would put the puzzle pieces together the way we did. He failed to erase the blackboard of his "Deckman" upbringing, and the military kept a record of his home address.

His brother, Lance, now lives in the same home they grew up in. He's an alcoholic. He owes money to the bank, has sold the equity in the house, has tried unsuccessfully three times for a small business loan, and was rejected on the grounds of bad personal credit. All of this information, supposedly private, Risina pulled from the Internet during our ride west. A natural fence, like I said.

The rain abates, so we approach the house. After a minute, a man in his early forties opens the door. He holds a beer bottle in one hand, and his eyes are droopy, red-rimmed, like a basset hound's.

"Help you?" he says as he takes a glance at me and then lets his gaze linger on Risina.

"Mr. Deckman?"

He turns back to me. "Yes?"

"Today's your lucky day."

He leans into the doorframe as his expression turns suspicious. I'm holding a duffel bag, and he eyes it, then looks back at me. "Hadn't had too many of those. What's the sale?"

"No sale. We're here to give you money. Can we come in?"

He folds his arms but doesn't budge.

"What's this about, pal?"

"It's about your brother."

"My brother?"

"Roland Deckman's your brother, correct?"

His eyes dart back and forth between us now, the lids pulled open. "Yes, but . . ."

"Well, he's made a significant amount of money over the last twenty years, and he wanted you to have most of it."

"Is he . . . has something happened to him?"

"Can we come in, sir? We'd rather not do this on the doorstep."

"Yes, of course." He blinks down at himself, tries to smooth out the wrinkles in his shirt, then props the door open, stepping aside. "Please, come in. Sorry . . . we get solicitors all the time here . . ."

"No problem."

Risina moves in first, and I follow. The house is a craftsman, lots of wood and rustic furniture. The living room is cramped and messy, like it hasn't had a wipe-down in a while. The television is on, a video game in mid-pause on the screen.

"Can I get you guys a beer? Or a . . . or some water?"

"No, we're fine, thank you."

We take seats on the sofa and Lance looks nervously at the screen and then presses a button on the remote so the television snaps to black.

After I let him stew for a moment, biting at the nail on his pinky finger, I lean forward. "I'll cut right to it then, Mr. Deckman. I don't know if your brother told you, but he was working for Central Intelligence."

"Yeah . . . he, uh, I don't know if I was supposed to know but he mentioned . . ."

"Good. It's certainly not against regulations."

I pause a moment longer, then smile sadly. "I'm sorry to say that your brother died in the line of duty."

I watch Lance's eyes, and they continue to move back and forth between us but don't cloud over. It's easy to see inside his head: he doesn't give a damn about his brother, he just wants to know what is in it for him. I suspect his credit cards are maxed out, his bills are piling up, and the house we're sitting inside is one of the few possessions he owns outright, paid for by his parents before they croaked.

He catches himself and coughs into his fist. "Oh . . . oh no. I . . . this is a shock, you know."

"I understand." I shift the duffel up to the coffee table, struggling for effect with the weight, and his eyes go to it like a prisoner looking at a key that fits his lock.

"Like I was saying, your brother socked away a significant sum during his employment, and his will states that he wants you to have it."

"How much?" He catches himself again. "I mean, wow, this is incredible. I'm . . ." He stops, coloring.

"Well, that's why we're here in person, Lance. This bag holds a hundred thousand dollars in cash . . ."

He's fun to watch. There's obvious disappointment at that amount—like it'll cover his debts but he isn't completely out of the woods. He won't be able to sit around playing video games for the rest of his life, all his bills paid. I keep playing with his emotions . . .

". . . which represents five percent of his wealth."

He swallows, and his lips purse and tremble like a baby with a pacifier. He's too dumb to do the math, but he knows the number has a lot of zeroes. I hand him the handles of the bag and he takes it in his lap. He wants to play it cool but he can't stop himself; he unzips the bag and looks over the stacks.

"Now here's the messy part."

His eyes dart up, searching my face. "Messy?"

"Yes, sir. See, we're authorized to release you the rest of the inheritance, but we need something from you before we can do that."

He nods before he even knows he's doing it. "Sure. What do you need?"

"Well, when an asset of ours dies, for national security reasons, we have to make sure all ties to him are erased. If an enemy were able to trace steps back to where he started, where he was living, where he kept personal possessions, files and such, we'd be . . . well, it would be bad for the country."

I have zero idea what I'm talking about, but I've read enough Ludlum, Clancy, and Follet to impersonate a government handler. Well, at least conjure enough of a performance to manipulate a desperate man who doesn't know jack shit.

"Yeah, sure. I understand." He stands up and absently wipes his hands on his shirt again. "Let me see . . ." He heads to a back hallway, leaving us alone in the living room.

Risina eyes me, a half smile on her face. I shrug, and we wait. I can hear doors open and close somewhere in the house, and then the sound of paper shuffling.

After a moment, Lance returns, holding a small yellow legal pad. In his other hand is a cell phone. He exhales loudly . . . "This is all I got. Umm . . . I haven't heard from Ro in years, shoot, I mean, had to be 2005 or so, after mom died. He had to sign some papers so I could, um, take over this place. He told me if I ever got in serious trouble, to, um . . . get ahold of him at this number."

He hands me the legal pad and the only thing scrawled on it is an 888 number. He hands me the phone. "He, uh, he said to use this phone so he'd know it was me. I guess it has a chip in it or something?" He hands me an old Nokia. "I haven't, uh, charged it in a while."

"Did you ever call him?"

"One time. I called him and some broad . . ." he looks over at Risina. "Sorry, I mean, some woman answered and said she was with some bank or something. At first, I thought I'd dialed the wrong number, then I realized it was probably a cover or something? I told her to tell Roland that his brother needed him.

"I swear it wasn't another five minutes and the phone rang in my hand. He was all concerned, out-of-breath you know, asking if I was in trouble. I told him I was running out of funds, you know . . . maybe he could loan me some money? He told me to only call him if my life was in danger, if someone had threatened me, that was it. That's the last I heard from him. We were never close, but I guess he . . . uh, I guess he . . ." He looks down at the duffel. ". . . wanted me to have a better life or something."

I stand up and Risina joins me. "You sure this is everything you have that could lead back to him? No address in Washington or anything?"

He holds up his empty hands, then crosses his arms like he's hugging himself. "No, nothing else. That's it. If he had a home address, he never gave it to me."

I nod, and look into his eyes, like I'm checking to see if he's lying when I already know he's telling the truth.

"Okay, Mr. Deckman. Thank you."

He looks at the duffel as we head to the door. "Sure, no problem." He follows us closely . . .

"So . . . the rest of the money?"

I stop, like I had forgotten about it. "Yes, sorry. My associate here will deliver it when we make sure there isn't any other way to get to your brother's identity through you."

"There isn't."

"I'm sure there isn't. It's just a formality. You mind if we give it to you in cash? Makes it cleaner for us."

"No, yeah, I mean, cash is great."

"Karen here will get back to you shortly. We, uh, we know where you live," I say with a laugh.

He laughs too, like he's relieved. As we step back off his stoop, "How . . . how did he die if you don't mind my asking?"

"It's classified," I offer, trying my best to look apologetic.

He nods again, then gives us a half wave, drops his hand like he was embarrassed about that, and then just shuts the door.

Risina and I climb in the car, and she chuckles. "Okay, not all of this job is miserable."

"No, not all of it," I agree as I hold up the phone. "Let's go find a place to call Decker and see if he might want to come say hello."

We take him at the casino.

Downtown Detroit has three of them, one in Greektown, and two in the middle of downtown. The MGM is a Vegas-style complex, with a full floor of gaming tables, restaurants, night-clubs and a show theater attached to a forty-story hotel.

I call the number from his phone and know it's going to be recorded, so I evince my best impression of his brother's nasally whine when the woman picks up with "National Investments."

"It's Lance. I'm outta money. And these guys at the MGM, they're not messing around. Tell my bro . . . tell Ro I gotta . . . I'm going in at midnight to room 4001 to meet these guys . . . just tell him I love him."

I hang up. The phone chirps in my hand three minutes later, but I ignore it. I don't remove the battery so they can pinpoint the location with whatever satellites do that type of thing. Since Risina and I are already checked into the hotel, it should paint a convincing picture.

I'm certain he'll come alone. He doesn't want his employers to know any more about his personal business than absolutely necessary, and certainly not about his deadbeat brother who got himself in a bad way with some casino heavies. No, my guess is he'll come in by himself, pissed off, armed but not ready to shoot, not ready to play defense. And as a man who understands the value of surprise, I'm betting he won't try to contact the casino owners ahead of time to straighten out this matter. If he does, my plan is sunk, but what better place to play the odds than right here in a gaming joint?

At eleven-thirty, Risina spots a man heading to the elevator, and after he gives it a cursory glance, he backtracks toward the reception area. His face is similar to his brother's, but better looking—a stronger jaw, brighter eyes—like the superior chromosomes bandied together to favor him and exclude his alcoholic brother. Still, the family resemblance is there.

The top floor requires an extra security card to trigger the elevator, so he'll have to request the floor, another indication this is our guy. Risina ducks in behind him, hears him request a room on the fortieth floor, and then listens to the receptionist give him room 4021.

He thanks her politely and heads back to the bank of elevators. I'm sure he's surging with grim energy, ready to confront the guys in room 4001 before his brother arrives, straighten out the situation, turn it ugly if he has to, whatever it takes to get his brother off the hook. After he presses the up button, the first doors to open are for the middle car in this deck of three, and as soon as he's in it, Risina calls up to me.

"Middle elevator, up now."

I'm on the twentieth floor. Above the doors are LCD readouts displaying the floor number of each car's current position. I watch and hit my own "up" button as the middle car passes the tenth floor. We tested this a few times and ten out of eleven, the elevator heading up is the one that stops; the only exception was when one of the other cars was already on the twentieth floor. But the right and left elevators are elsewhere and the one rising should be the correct choice, come on. Except now as I look, the elevator up on twenty-eight is heading down this direction and if it gets here first, I don't know what will happen, which door will open. The middle one continues to climb, please don't let someone else in the teens press "up" and stop it. It's moving up steadily, 17, 18 . . . while the one on the right continues to fall, 22, 21, and then it hits 20 and I hold my breath, but it keeps heading down, 19, 18 on the way to the lobby and then the middle elevator door dings open. No one else is inside but Decker. I have a ball cap slung low so he won't get a good look at me. I doubt he knows my face but if he's working closely with Spilatro, I can't be sure.

I move in quickly, pull my card out to clear security for the top floor, then shrug since the 40 button is already lit up. I move to the back wall as the doors close, hoping he'll scoot up but he's experienced enough to keep his back to the wall. I have a burnt cigar in my mouth to mask the smell of what I'm about to do.

This is different from my usual work, an anomaly because I don't want Decker dead. If this had been an assignment, I would have popped him when the door opened. But I want him alive, unconscious. My left hand drops to my pocket, where the handkerchief soaked in chloroform rests. I can see him in my periphery, and he definitely checks me out as the elevator crosses 30 on its way to the top.

I have about ten more seconds to do this. I hope the smell doesn't give me away, but the cigar's scent is strong and should overpower the chemicals.

The elevator passes 34. I have eight more seconds, maybe five, but before I can pull out the rag, he says, "Do I know you?" and I can feel the pressure of a handgun's barrel pressed against my temple. He's a professional, a *government* professional, and he's trained to spot anomalies like warning flags, so a guy on twenty pressing forty must stand out. He may not know I'm Columbus, but he knows I'm someone sent to shadow him, and he probably mistakes me for one of the guys who is about to hold his brother in room 4001.

The elevator chimes as the floor hits forty and in that little jostle elevator cars make when they come to a rest, I duck the gun and drive my forehead into his chin. He jerks back instinctively, and I pin his arm to the wall, the one fisting the gun, and I bang it one, two times into the back paneling and the gun drops. Unfortunately, by focusing my energy on the gun, my rib cage is vulnerable, and he takes advantage, pounding me in the side with his free fist, just as the door springs open.

He's a strong puncher, even in close quarters, and he connects in my kidney with a rabbit punch that doubles me over. He drops for the gun but I'm able to kick it out the open door onto the fortieth floor hallway and luckily, no one is up here waiting to catch a ride down. The door starts to shut on us, and he dives for the gun, but I grab his leg and the door bangs into him before springing open again. He kicks backward at me and connects with his heel to my chest before he dives for his gun in the hallway.

I leap for him. If he gets to that gun first, I'm sunk and this whole damn thing is for naught. I won't let that happen, can't let that happen. He's on the gun, but I'm on him, and before he can roll over and come up with it, I drive my fist into the crook of his elbow, snapping his arm backward. The elevator behind us closes and heads down again, leaving us to battle it out here in the fortieth floor foyer. I can see another car heading up this way, in the thirties and climbing. If it's coming to this floor, we're going to be spotted and who knows how quickly security will be here next. Somebody might have heard the scuffle and the hotel dicks are already on the way.

Unexpectedly, Deckman or Decker or whatever-the-fuck-his-name-is works his legs around my mid-section and squeezes my torso in a scissor-lock. I've seen mixed martial artists do this shit on TV, but it's a new one to me. Before I know it, he's forced me off of him, and I can barely breathe, barely move my arms as he squeezes the air out of my lungs. At the same time, he gropes with his hands, reaching behind him for the gun on the ground . . .

The elevator continues to climb toward our floor, 35, 36, but the numbers are going fuzzy, like I'm looking at them through a kaleidoscope. I pound my elbows into his thighs, but the muscles there are like rocks.

He keeps pulling us backward, just a few feet from his gun now, and if I'm going to make a move, it's going to have to be in that last instant, when he reaches for his pistol and releases just a little bit of pressure from my ribs.

We slide another few inches and I'm able to reach my hand into my pocket and withdraw that cloth. The numbers above the door pass 39 and that car is coming and whatever he or I plan to do, it's going to be in front of witnesses. He drags us the last few inches and his hands seize on that pistol, a little Colt .22, and the pressure from his legs around my waist loosens only a bit. We both twist around at the same time, toward each other, just as the elevator dings, and he swivels with the gun as I swivel with the cloth, but I'm a half-second faster and I mash that cloth into his face and hold it there, pin it there, up under his nose and mouth. He bucks wildly but doesn't fire that pistol and his eyes roll to the back of his head as his whole body goes slack, and his legs finally drop from my waist.

"You all right?" Risina says, stepping out of the elevator car, a Glock in her hand. I'm glad I was a half-second quicker or she might have witnessed something a bit bloodier when she emerged onto the floor.

"He's checked into 4021," she says as she stoops over his limp body and withdraws his key card.

"Then let's show him to his room," I grunt as I wrestle him up.

No sooner do we have him propped between us than a maid rounds the corner, pushing a cart. She barely glances our way as she moves down the hall. He's not the first semi-conscious guest she has encountered in the hallway and won't be the last, I'm sure. Probably not even tonight.

# CHAPTER ELEVEN

He comes out of it talking. My guess is he's been conscious long before he opened his eyes. He was hoping we would give something away while he pretended to be sawing logs, but his patience went unrewarded.

I sit in a metal folding chair in front of him. I hit him with a full wet rag of chloroform—hell, I almost passed out just soaking the cloth—so I estimated we had a couple of hours to make arrangements. We bribed a member of the hotel's security to take us down the service elevator and get us to our car in the garage. Five thousand dollars and a story about a Motown record producer who tripped himself stupid got us a wheelchair, an escort, and no questions. The lethargic guard might not have bought it from me, but one look at Risina sold the story.

It only took twenty minutes of driving around downtown for us to find what we were looking for: an abandoned warehouse. Shit, you could put on a blindfold and walk around downtown Detroit in any direction and find one. A cursory reconnaissance of the place yielded no derelicts and no security.

So when Deckman finally opens his eyes, it's the three of us alone, and with his arms and legs fastened tightly, like I said, he wants to talk.

"You have no idea who you guys are fucking with. If you touch one hair on my brother's head, I will open up a hurricane of destruction on you and your operation you can only dream of."

I just stare at him with somnolent eyes, like I'm somewhere between amused and bored.

"Where is he? Where are you holding my brother?"

Still, I give him nothing, just let him get himself worked up.

"You might intimidate a lot of people with that thousand-yard-stare, tough guy, but I guarantee you are wasting it on me. We can talk and figure this business out together or you might as well pop me and get it over with, because the more you make me wait, the less lenient I'm going to be when we meet up later under different circumstances."

"I could give two shits about your brother."

He grins. "That makes two of us. You got a cigarette I can bum?"

I just shake my head and he shrugs like it was worth a shot to ask for one. I wait for him to strain at his bindings again, testing out their tensile strength. He gives up after a moment, and I lean forward.

"I want to know how to contact Spilatro."

Some hitters like to use their fists to elicit information, try to break a man so he'll pour out his secrets, like punching a hole in the bottom of a water bucket. Not me. Like Kirschenbaum did to me in that hotel room in Connecticut, I stagger Deckman by playing with his expectations.

The name "Spilatro" floors him, like a driver who has to jerk the wheel suddenly when an animal darts into the road.

"I don't know what you're talking about."

I let him dangle.

After a moment, he sighs and looks up at the ceiling. "You're the guy, huh? The one he's gone on about?"

"I'm the guy."

"Columbus."

"That's right."

"So you kidnapped me to get to him."

"Means to an end."

He nods. "So now what?"

"A swap. You for my friend."

"Oh, yeah. The pistol."

"Pistol?"

"Black guy in Chicago. Pulled a .22 from under his mattress. Name was Grant but we'll always call him the Pistol after that."

"That's right," I say, and I'm oddly comforted that Archie impressed them enough to earn a new nickname. "Spilatro had two guys there."

"Three, actually. And Spilatro never left the lobby. Pretty straightforward snatch-and-grab except your friend pops up with that pea-shooter right as I get my knee into his back. He squeezed a round off at Bando but missed his head by six inches—I pried the gun away from him after that." He spits on to the dirty cement next to his feet, making a clear mark in the dust. "That scrawny dog could put up a fight. I'll give him that."

"Who broke his nose?"

"Who cares?"

"Little payback from Bando?"

"Does it matter?"

I let that one sail by.

"How long have you and Spilatro been government guys?"

He looks at me sideways. "Who sold you that dope?"

"Two and two makes four."

"Except you put the wrong numbers into the calculator."

"Did I?"

Deckman shrugs. "Who's the chick?" he asks as he cranes his neck to get an eye on Risina.

"Man in your position might choose his words more carefully."

"I haven't felt this terrified since my dad got out his belt," he says flatly.

"Your dad in Northville?"

"My dad six feet under in Birmingham."

"That's right. It's your brother in Northville."

"You hurt him?"

I shake my head.

"Sure I can't have a smoke?"

I shake it again and he grins. "How'd you get Lance to give me up?"

"I told him you were dead. Said you left him some money."

He nods. "Dollar signs was all it took, huh? Surprised you were the first to try it. He tell you I was a government man?"

"I already knew it."

"Uh-huh. He's my kid brother. You think I'm gonna tell him I plug guys for money?"

"I don't care what you tell him."

He falls silent for a moment. Then lifts his chin again, "You gonna let me—"

I interrupt to throw a wrench in his tactics. "How do we get ahold of your army buddy?"

He snickers, like this is all too much for him. "You're not fishing. I can tell that. You must have a full file on me."

"I had to pick up a new fence since you snatched mine."

Risina smiles at that. She's behind Deckman, so he doesn't notice. I repeat, "How do I contact Spilatro?"

"You got my phone?"

"What's the number?"

"Give me my phone and then give me my hands. I'll track him down for you."

"Your phone is smashed and in a trash can in the parking garage at the MGM. Along with your two pistols and the knife you had in that cute little wrist sheath."

This gets him to draw in his smirk. "Doesn't matter. They'll know where I was last."

"Who will?"

"You'll find out."

"Will I? It's a big city."

He shrugs, looks down at the floor. He tries to toe that spit mark he made in the dust, but can't get to it with his foot.

I haven't broken his confidence, but chipped at it, like a ship cracking through ice to get to the pole. I sit back and fold my hands behind my head. "Tell me about the dark men."

His eyelids flutter, slightly. Then, he offers, "I gotta go to the can."

I don't move, just keep the chain tethered between our eyes.

"You gonna make me piss myself?"

"You can earn trips to the bathroom."

"You'd fit right in at Abu Ghraib."

"I'll take your word for it."

He takes another run at the bindings then settles again to see if he accomplished any slack. He grunts, unsatisfied, then does that thing people do when they're absently thinking. He sort of moves his lips over to the side of his face. After a moment, he looks up again. "All right then. How you wanna play this? Because I'm getting bored and quite frankly, a little angry."

"Tell us how to bring Spilatro out, and this can end lickety-split."

"What if I don't?"

"I'm not going to shoot you, or beat you, or cut you, if that's what you're wondering. I always thought that was more of a weasel play, and I don't care for it, to tell you the truth. I mean, if you want immediate results, it's probably the way to go, cut a man up, get him to talk, but why go to the trouble when I have nothing but time? So what I'm going to do is sit behind you in the dark back there and watch you die of thirst."

He stares at me evenly, his face hot, as he tries to gauge whether or not I mean what I say.

Risina walks over and hands me a fast-food bag. I take out a plastic bottle of water, take a swig, then set the remainder in my chair.

"I checked online, and the maximum someone can go without water is ten days. But the statistics say your body will pretty much shut down in three. Three days? Can you imagine? That's nothing. That's a weekend. That's a 'hey, I've got plans on Tuesday so I'll see you on Wednesday.'"

Risina pulls up a camera and takes a picture of him. Then we leave him there to think about that water bottle just out of his reach, Tantalus with his grapes.

This place must've once been some sort of manufacturing plant servicing the auto industry, but it has the look of a place run-down long before the Big Three started asking for government handouts.

An office adjacent to the room provides a window that looks out onto the front of the building so I can spot any unwelcome vehicles approaching. Whoever owns this warehouse doesn't keep a regular security guard here, but maybe he pays someone to come out and look around once a week or once a month, the way Bacino's neighbor did back in Chicago. It doesn't look like the front door has been cracked in years, and I'm happy to keep playing the percentages, but if someone does happen to roll snake eyes, I'd like to have a few minutes warning to get my money off the table.

The room has another window on the opposite wall that faces the back of Deckman's chair. He spent the first hour trying to tip the chair, and the second hour yelling just to yell. The next morning, he's stiff and sore and broken. It didn't take long.

"You kept in your piss. I'm proud of you."

"Fuck you," he croaks.

I start to stand again, and I can see the desperation in his eyes as clear as if I can read his thoughts. I'm going to guess he's never been tortured before, neither during the first Gulf War nor at any point in his professional life, because he doesn't have the mettle to test his own durability.

"Okay, listen. I don't know why we gotta play it like this." His voice sounds scratchy, like a rake on the sidewalk.

"Tell me how to contact him."

"Okay, but listen. Here's the thing." His eyes ping-pong between my face and the water bottle in the chair. "You're a dead man. You have to understand this. I say this not to be confrontational, but it's a fact, as sure as these walls are white or that floor is cement. As sure as I can admit you know what you're doing in tying a man to a chair. Spilatro is the smartest man I know, the smartest I've ever known. He thinks *differently*, you see? He sees the world as interconnected lines, or, or, dominoes toppling against each other . . . but *he* sets 'em up, you see? He cuts the lines. He knows exactly which pieces are going to fall when, because everything fits into the little designs, the patterns he creates. We're the dominoes, man. And he's the finger pushing 'em over.

"He was always better than me. It wasn't even a competition. He has this disconnect thing he can do where he just shuts it all off, any compassion, any concern for innocents, anything that stands in the way of the dominoes falling. He's already played this out, man. You just don't know it."

"If that's true, then he gave you up like a pawn on a chessboard."

"Did he? I don't know. You can't look at the micro with him. Just the macro."

"So he's expecting my call?"

"I'm sure he is. Which is why I don't really feel like sticking out this 'dying of thirst' scenario. Let's get on with it. Give me some water and I'll tell you how to get to him."

"Was he expecting me to kill you?"

His throat bobs. "What's that?"

I pull out my Glock and enunciate slowly. "Was he expecting me to kill you?"

His mouth moves to the side of his face again. "I don't think the percentage play is to do that if you want your friend back. I'm sure that's why we didn't dump what's-his name, Pistol, in the Chicago River. There's an exchange to be made. That's why we did it."

"But if I shoot you now, it'll throw Spilatro off his game, right?"

"If you shoot me now, your friend is dead."

I don't look at Risina. I told her she'd have to see this side of me and that she might not like it. But this is the game. This is the difference between talking about it and doing it, the difference between theory and application, the difference between looking at a photo of a crime scene and having another man's blood on your face, your hands. They brought the fight to us and that's where the truth lies. I hope she can see the difference. There is an entire universe in the difference.

"Maybe. All I know is if he was expecting me to take you and make an exchange, as you figure, then the best play for me is to kill you and disrupt his plans."

"But you still don't know how to contact him."

"Then tell me."

His eyes dart wildly, like a wild animal that wants the food in your right hand but is worried about the left hand he can't see behind your back.

"If I tell you, how do I know you won't kill me?"

"You'll have to wait and see."

"Not good enough."

"I thought you wanted to end this. I thought Spilatro already knew how this was going to play out. One way or another, I'm going to confront him, either pretending I have you to trade, or physically having you to trade. Like I said, I have nothing but time.

"So we have three choices here. One, we can go back to the thirst scenario and see how you're doing tomorrow. Two, you can give me the number and hope for the best. And three, I can shoot you and figure out another way to contact Spilatro, maybe a way he hasn't figured yet."

"That's what I'm telling you . . . he's figured all three plays! He knows what you're going to do. There's no free will here. Not with him!"

I pick up the water bottle, untwist the lid, and then take another swallow, so now the bottle is only half-full. "All right then," I say, setting the bottle back on the chair. "See you tomorrow."

I only take two steps before he says, "Wait."

Thirty seconds later, he gives me the number to reach Spilatro. I take off the lid to the water bottle and hold it to his lips. He gulps it down in three swallows. While the bottle is to his lips, I put my Glock to the side of his head and fire once.

I suppose there was a fourth play, the one where he tells me what I want to know, and I shoot him anyway.

She's in the bathroom, throwing up. I give her a lot of credit. She put up a brave face for a long time, but the reality of what I do for a living, what I've always done, caught up to her in this empty warehouse on the west side of downtown Detroit. I'm not going to try to talk to her through the closed bathroom door, though I have a lot to say. I do know the sooner we get out of here, the better I'll feel. While she jerked her head at the concussive sound of the pop, her face bloodless as she saw Deckman's head explode, and then turned on her heels to hightail it to the bathroom, I picked up the body and dragged it behind a rusted and forgotten drill press. Deckman kept his frame fit, so it wasn't too difficult to move him. I saw the bathroom door slam shut out of the corner of my eye as I finished disposing of the body.

I hear the water running in the sink. It hasn't stopped running. I imagine she's checking herself in the mirror, searching for a visible change in her face. After a moment, the door opens and she emerges, ashen.

"I'm sorry for this," she says, chewing on a breath mint. "I . . ."

"It had to be done, Risina."

"I know. It's just . . ."

"We couldn't try to transport him. The longer you keep a prisoner around, the more chances he has to disrupt your assignment. And this is an assignment, Risina. I've been ducking that mentally for a while, but make no mistake about it, it's an assignment. The name at the top of the page is Spilatro. After we deal with him, we figure the rest of it out."

"I understand. I need to get some air, if you don't mind, before I vomit again."

I can't tell if she's agreeing with me because she processes what I'm saying or if she's trying to block it from her mind.

We find the side door and the crisp air envelops us, sweeping away the smell of dust and death in the warehouse. I parked our sedan around the side of the place so it wouldn't be visible from the street.

Before she can open the passenger door, I move over to hold her and she submits, burying her face in my chest.

"I was done, Risina. You know that. And then they came to us. They took Archie and penned a note with my name on it and forced me to answer it. These aren't innocent men."

"I know," she says, her face hidden. Her eyes weren't red when she emerged from the bathroom and she's not crying now.

"You going to be okay?"

"Yes."

She reaches up and kisses me on the cheek, but it's perfunctory, devoid of feeling. "We should leave, yes?"

"Yes."

She slides into the passenger seat, and I get behind the wheel, crank the engine. In two minutes, we roll away from the broken chain link gate. Another ten and we're on the highway heading east. Another twenty and Risina's asleep, the last forty-eight hours sapping her energy like physical blows.

I don't know if her attitude toward me will change now that she's stepped behind the curtain and seen me unmasked. I told her once I was a bad man, but up until this morning, they were only words.

# CHAPTER TWELVE

T he blossoms have fallen off the cherry trees as we return
to Washington. Discarded cotton candy mounds mark
every few feet as sidewalk sweepers push the petals into
piles. Trees we were admiring just a week ago now look bald
and empty. It happens that quickly.

"Why didn't you tell me?"

"Tell you what?"

We've set up camp in a budget hotel on the outskirts of
McLean, Virginia, near the location of the CIA headquarters.
I'm looking to disrupt Spilatro's operating method any way I
can. I've already put a bullet in the head of his oldest friend,
now I'm going to approach him in his own back yard, see if I
can shake the leaves from his trees.

"Tell me that you were going to shoot him after he gave you
the number."

"I knew it had to be done from the moment we kidnapped
him in the hotel. You can't keep a wild dog chained to you for
too long if you don't want to be bit. I didn't know how you'd
react and honestly, didn't want to have an argument about it.

I wanted you to be a part of it, but I didn't want you to give anything away if you knew. If he saw it in your eyes, I might not have gotten the information from him. It was a delicate tightrope—"

"You didn't trust me."

"No, that's not it. Trust has nothing to do with it. It's only a matter of the unknown, and as a contract killer, you have to keep the unknown at bay every chance you get. That's the job. I didn't know how you'd react, and I knew what needed to happen. Once I killed him, it wouldn't matter how you reacted."

"Well, you should have told me anyway. You should have dealt with my reaction up front instead of catching me by surprise."

"I'm not going to apologize for this, Risina. I had to play the cards dealt to me."

She folds her arms across her chest and glares at me, grimacing.

"I'm in this all the way with you," she starts. "You need to be in all the way with me."

"I am."

"No. You're lying to yourself about that. I've known it since Smoke died in Chicago and you saw you couldn't protect him. He died in the worst way possible, right in front of us. And since that moment—"

"Risina . . ."

"Let me finish. Since that moment, you've known it could happen to me too. So you won't let yourself be in all the way with me. You've been questioning bringing me with you from the beginning."

I'm practiced at keeping my face blank, but it's as open as a book right now, and she reads it, reads that she's right.

Her voice catches, but she plows forward, her Italian accent thickening with every word. "So listen to me and listen carefully. I'm not going away. I'm not leaving you. And you may not be able to protect me. I might get hurt or worse, but as you say, those are the cards we've been dealt. If the plan is to kill someone to get us to the point we need, then tell me. If the plan is to use me as bait the way you did in Rome with Svoboda, then tell me. Jesus Christ, just tell me. Quit trying to do everything alone. We're partners. We're a tandem, as you call it. Just tell me."

"Okay."

She starts to protest, so sure I am going to argue the point. "Okay?"

"Yes. You're right. You're right about everything. I brought you along because you were in danger the moment Smoke found us. I thought there was a better chance I could keep you safe if you were with me than if I left you behind or stashed you somewhere. I didn't want you showing up in a photograph holding a newspaper with your mouth gagged and your hands tied behind your back, someone using you to break me."

"I know what you are. I know your fearful symmetry, okay? I've known all along and I am a part of it, yes? The same hand that dared seize the fire to create you, created me.

"I've realized something about us. Something I think pro-found. Not because it's a clever thought, but just because it *is*. You walked into my bookshop in Rome and I didn't change you. You changed *me*. There is no changing you. Like a beast hibernating, you went dormant when we were on the island, but you didn't change."

"I didn't mean for this to—"

"You don't understand what I'm saying. I want you to know you changed me, but I needed to change. Some of us don't find out who we are or what we are until another comes along to liberate us from the cages we build for ourselves. You did that to me. You liberated me."

I stand up and move to her chair, hold out my hand and pull her into me. "But what if you don't like the change? What if you discover you were happier before?"

"I was dead before."

And then, as if to prove her point, she spends the next hour making us both feel alive.

He answers on the third ring.

"Hello?" It is unmistakably his voice, the same one I heard in the rented house in upstate New York. It has an enunciated sibilance to it that is as unique as a fingerprint.

"You have something I want."

He stops breathing, presumably deciding whether he should hang up to regroup or plow forward. I've called him on his private phone, touched him when he thought he was the only one doing the touching. He pauses a moment, and that moment tells me everything—I have, in fact, disrupted his plan.

"Good. I was expecting your call. I'm surprised it took you this long."

"You know, everyone keeps telling me how smart you are. Including you. But now I'm starting to wonder . . ."

"Okay. Okay," he stammers.

Rattling him is easier than I imagined. I can picture him on the other end of the line, his face contorting the way it did when he found his wife standing next to his model of Cleveland. He doesn't care for surprises; that part of the story was true. I wonder what miniature mousetrap he's constructed for me and how worthless it is to him now.

"Okay," he says for the third time. "You come to me, and I'll release Mr. Grant."

"Like a rat sniffing cheese while a steel bar snaps his neck?"

"You're starting to get the idea."

"You want to exchange me for my friend?"

"I want you to come willingly. Your friend is immaterial."

"You know who else is immaterial? A soldier you used to run with. Roland Deckman. He's gone by 'Decker' for the last twenty years or so."

Spilatro pauses, then starts laughing. There's an undercurrent to the sound though, like a stage laugh. It's strained, wrong. "I assume that'd be the way you'd locate me. I tried to teach him, to give him advice, but he wouldn't listen. Some people in this game think they're invincible."

"So now I have something you want."

"I don't give a damn about Roland Deckman."

"You have twelve hours or he dies."

"Right."

"Check your phone."

I press "send" on the picture that Risina took when Deckman was tied and alive.

"I'm not going to tell you you're bluffing, because I don't think you are. I just don't think you've thought this through. If you kill Decker . . ."

"What I haven't done is given you time to think it through. Twelve hours. I'll call you again on this phone with the meeting place two hours before. Have Archie ready to move."

"You're making a mistake."

"Just correcting one."

"You'll have to give me more time if you want Mr. Grant in one piece."

"Twelve hours."

He hesitates again. Then, "Where are you calling from?"

"Some place close."

Walking to the car with Risina, I'm pleased. All conversations are about exchanging information, and when dealing with a mark, you try to get more than you give. Spilatro gave away something with his question at the end.

He's a government hitter all right, and he's working for these dark men, as he said, but this job isn't sanctioned. It isn't authorized. He doesn't have a support team or a gaggle of analysts helping him break it down. If he were working through proper channels, he would've immediately known where I was calling from, probably had it pinpointed within a few city blocks. The playing field is leveled in a way. Nonetheless, I place the phone under my right rear tire before I pull away from the hotel.

How do you disrupt someone who thinks he can game out every move? When Kasparov played Deep Blue in their infamous chess match of 1996, he beat the machine by charging illogically at the beginning of each match, then set up random traps to capitalize on the computer's hesitancy.

I'm going to charge illogically at Spilatro.

He's made a mistake: he thinks I care about Archie Grant. He thinks the kidnapping of my friend, of my fence, is why I came back. He thinks that's why I'm holding Decker. He thinks I actually care about an exchange.

It was my *name*. He put my name on a sheet of paper and called me out. No matter who instructed him, who gave him the assignment to kill me, he's the one who put that note where Smoke would find it. He wrote my name on that paper and the machine was set into motion. It'll only stop moving when he's dead.

There's not going to be an exchange, a negotiation. Not because I've already killed Decker, but because I don't really care if Grant dies too. Sure, I'd rather he came out of this alive, but that would be a bonus, rather than the point.

I'm going to kill Spilatro as soon as I spot him. No talking, no give-and-take, just pull up my gun and shoot him in the head.

I tell this to Risina as we drive down a Virginia road, strip malls and shopping centers breaking up the horizon. Her hands are on her knees, knitted together.

"You said you wanted to know the plan. That's the plan."

"You don't care about Archie? This has never been about Archie?"

"I like him. He's a good fence. A great one, even. And I liked his sister very much, too. But if he dies in the middle of this, or if he's already dead? I won't mourn him. I won't think about him. And he wouldn't mourn me either. You wanted to see me, Risina, to see the real me? This is who I am."

She nods. "You just shut off your feelings?"

"About everyone and everything except you. And I let my rage build for the man I have to kill. But don't let rage and rashness blend. My rage allows me to take a man's life and walk away from it cleanly, but I am never rash in executing the hit. Cold-blooded *and* cold-hearted, you have to be both."

"And powerful, yes?"

"Power is the drug that hooks you to this job. Ending some-one's life against his will—it's something you can't fathom until you do it. It takes an even greater hold of you when you know you do it well, when you plan it and execute it and get away with it. My first fence told me it was a power reserved for God, and there is an attraction in that power that is difficult to resist."

"And Archie? How did he deal with this power?"

"If he does his job right, he sets up his hitters' successes. He compiles the information and hints at the best strategies. He lays out the evil in the target for his killers so they can stoke that rage. A hit man has to connect with the evil so he can sever the connection, and a good fence knows this, knows the impor-tance of this. He does the plotting without the bloodshed. It's a different power the fence holds, but I'm sure the good ones share in it."

"When we finish this, I want to be your fence."

She says it in such a matter-of-fact way that I can tell she's been thinking about it for a while. "Even if we get Archie out alive?"

"Even then."

"But we could run again. Hide out. Find a new spot, somewhere even more remote."

"No. You know we would just wait for the next man to come. There will always be a next man who comes."

"I wanted to believe in a future without this."

"You can't have it, any more than a tiger can lie in a cage and forget his instincts."

She's right. She has a way of getting inside my head and saying things I won't let myself think.

"But why would you want to do this with me?"

"Because we are good together. Because I think I was born to do this work. Because I would like to know that you have every piece of information at your disposal to be successful. Because I can provide that, make the file come to life. Live, breathe. It's research, it's writing, but it has to have heart. For you to be the person you are, it has to have heart. I read all those files in Archie's office and it was like discovering a new library that no one knew existed. It was life and death and love and pain and beauty and horror in one place, in those pages, and it was riveting. Biblical. I can do that. I can put it all together for you. Only for you. And better than Archie. I need time to learn, but yes, better than Archie."

"You sound certain."

"I am."

"Where would we live?"

"The place you and I both know best. Boston."

"And how would you establish us there?"

"You still know a few people. Word will spread quickly that Columbus is back in the business."

"And how will you protect yourself?"

"We'll protect each other. A pair of tigers, burning bright."

She grins, pleased with her idea. Maybe it can work, if we survive the day.

I tell Spilatro an address near the Potomac just outside the District in an industrial area. Canneries rise out of the landscape, monstrous, noisy and bleak. It's as though men couldn't stand to look at the beauty of a river cutting through a fertile countryside and so did all in their power to poison the land.

I demanded the exchange take place at seven-thirty, when the sun hangs low and the commercial district will be primarily unpopulated. We might have to deal with security guards and cameras pointed at the street, but I don't care. I'm finishing it now.

I want to drop Risina off at a coffee shop and pick her up when it's over, but she refuses. I tell her that fences don't participate in kills, and she tells me she isn't my fence until this is over. The thought of not knowing what is happening while she sips on a decaf latté is more than she can bear. She's been in this one since the beginning and she'll be in it until the end, and if she sees the dark side of me again standing over Spilatro's dead body, then she welcomes it.

I told Spilatro the address and he tried to keep me on the line, but I didn't give him the opportunity. He's learned all he's going to learn about me, and now the preparation is over and the two killers have to take the field until one is dead.

A black Toyota Tercel with tinted windows slowly rolls to a nearby intersection, the address I gave him, and then turns right and speeds away. I expect to see the same car again soon

. . . he came fifteen minutes early to get the lay of the land, do some reconnaissance. I haven't given him time to set up a mousetrap. He's in my world, the world of improvisation, a world he can't control, a world where he has to take advantage of the opportunities as they develop or die face-down in the street.

"This is it. I'm moving out. When you see the muzzle flash, race in and pick me up. Don't hesitate."

She nods and I kiss her and I think she says "be careful," but it's lost in the wind as I duck low out of the passenger side and move to a row of shrubs. I didn't anticipate how quickly the wind could pick up this close to the river and there's an industrial smell to the air, that combination of gas and oil and chemicals that seems to linger around factories like a trip wire: "Don't cross here or you'll cough up blood."

The shrubs line a concrete barrier demarking the property of a sardine cannery, and I slip between the greenery and the wall to make my way down to the intersection.

The sky turns that deep sea green as the sun hides in the horizon, and the traffic on the street is minimal, a few trucks rolling out of factories and lumbering up the streets. I find a spot where the intersection is visible through a break in the branches, and here comes that Tercel. I'm going to show myself just long enough for him to step out of the car and ask about the exchange so I can pop him in the head.

Two hundred yards away and it's impossible to see if he has Archie in the car with him, and if he does, I'll do my best to save my old fence, but only once the job is done and Spilatro is down and I can get away clean. Only then.

One hundred yards now and my Glock is out and in my hand. The wind howls, whistling a dirge as it crests the concrete barrier and zips through the shrubbery. Fifty yards.

Out of nowhere, a taxi smashes into the side of the Tercel and drives it across the width of the street, up on to the opposite sidewalk. The section of the Tercel from the driver's side tire to the door is bent concave from the force of the taxi's bumper and the engine has caught fire and whatever play this is . . . I have no idea what he's up to, but it has to be a play.

I can feel the advantage shifting between us, or is that adrenaline in my system? I have to decide how to make a move and what move to make, goddam him.

The taxi driver gets out of the car, a middle-easterner with a tight turban and a full beard, and he's yelling at the driver of the Tercel, and what the hell play can this be in the small amount of time I've given him? What am I walking into?

The door to the Tercel somehow swings open and a man climbs out but he isn't Spilatro, at least he doesn't look like Spilatro, not exactly, he looks too young from this angle, but can I be sure? He's dangling a gun at his side, and as the taxi driver registers this and starts to wave his hands and turn around saying "no, no, no, no, no," the driver shoots him in the back, BAM, dropping him in the road, just another piece of debris from the accident. Through the open door of the Tercel, I can see a figure slumped in the backseat, a dark figure, maybe it's Archie, fuck, this is not what I was expecting. The fire from the hood starts to vomit clouds of black smoke, whipped into a frenzy by the wind and someone nearby, some security guard or late-leaving lunch-bucket union douchebag must've heard the collision or is going to spot the smoke and dial 9-1-1 and then everything I've put into this moment is going to spoil like weeks-old bread. I'm going to have to bite, now.

When I kill, I don't like dropping anyone collaterally, anyone besides my target, because things get messy, but this isn't a target, not really, they targeted me, and if he enlisted some of these dark men, some other hitters the way he did Deckman with his wife's gambit, then they're going to join him lying on the pavement. What's real and what's not is what has had me on my heels this whole time but I have to move in and shift the advantage back to my favor.

I walk quickly from the shrubs and make my way toward the accident, toward the shooter who might be Spilatro but doesn't look like the man I saw two times, and he spots me coming.

"Where's Decker?" he says in a voice I don't recognize—he's not Spilatro—this only takes a moment to register, but he raises his weapon like a Western gunslinger and I already have mine up and fire from thirty yards away, catch him in the forehead and spin him like a top.

I step past the dead cab driver and the dead Tercel driver and head to the sedan, and the guy in the backseat, the one I thought was Archie blows a hole out the window. A bullet whizzes close enough to my ear to make my lobe flap like laundry drying in the wind, and I duck behind the car, lucky the bullet didn't rip my head off.

The man squirms in his seat as he tries to find me and when he turns to the back windshield, I'm already there, in his blind spot. I fire and the back windshield shatters along with half the man's face. He didn't adjust for the fraction of an inch the glass between us would make on his shot. I didn't make the same mistake.

"We have her!" says a voice to my right, and when I wheel, the cab driver is up off the pavement, up and alive and glaring at me, a pistol aimed my way. And now I see it. The beard is fake and the turban is covering a bald head and the bullet he took in the back was staged and the voice is that same prissy "I'm smarter than you" whine I've heard before except there's a desperation anchoring it down to the pavement like an albatross around his neck.

I didn't give him time to prepare and the best he could come up with on the fly was a faux wreck attached to a shell game and his hitters were dealt the dummy hand and are dead before they even knew what game they were playing. I imagine Bando is one of them, the clown who broke Archie's nose for having the audacity to put up a fight in his own bedroom and now he's either the one dead on the pavement or the one dead in the backseat of the Tercel. Spilatro thought I'd walk up and talk and he could plug me from behind but he didn't count on my Glock speaking for me.

His words stop me though. His plan had a wild card, a joker. "We have her" and I look up the street and sure enough, Risina is out of the driver's side with a gun to her head.

Holding the pistol is Carla.

Carla, who I listened to for hours as she poured her heart out regarding her husband's betrayal, whom I believed whole-heartedly, whose story I swallowed like a spoonful of fucking ice cream and maybe that's the part I misjudged the most about my rust, my diminished abilities. I thought my killing skills had dropped, the physical skills, but it's the mental part that has to be exercised to stay finely tuned . . . the ability to read faces, gestures, voices, lies. I thought I was in shape, but I'm faced with my failure now; I was played like a fool and my sand castle crashed down, stomped on by the ugly woman with the hound-dog face and the black heart.

She's too far away to attempt a shot and Spilatro sneers as he aims his gun in my direction.

"What say we all get in the car and take a trip?"

He gestures toward the taxi.

"I thought you didn't like confrontation up close and personal."

"You shouldn't believe everything you hear from hostile witnesses."

I nod, the Glock heavy in my hand.

Spilatro smiles, his voice hitting that fingernails-on-a-chalk-board pitch. "I told you I was smarter than—"

I shoot him in the head, the bullet slamming into his right eye.

His gun goes off, a finger spasm, but I don't hear it, don't even wait to see Spilatro drop. My mental game may be lagging but my ability to hit a man at fifteen feet will never flag, and I sprint directly at Carla, my focus on only her, as everything else fades away. I don't feel the pavement under my feet, don't feel the wind in my face, don't feel the wetness searing the edges of my eyes. She's far away, too far away, why did I park so fucking far? Why did I bring Risina? Why didn't I—

Carla blanches, then shoves Risina into the car and is behind the wheel and I see her cold-cock Risina with the butt of her gun, one, two, three times, wham, wham, wham, a blur, a whipsaw, and Risina's face is bloody and out and she's slumped and the engine cranks and I shoot into the windshield which spiders but the car launches into a left turn, tires screaming, engine thundering.

Only then do I realize I'm bleeding, shot in the chest by Spilatro's involuntary finger jerk.

I don't know how to . . . won't know how to find her if she escapes with Risina.

Wheeling on a dime, I sprint back to the taxi with the damaged front end, the old Crown Vic that Spilatro drove into the Tercel, and I'm in the driver's seat and behind the wheel and the engine is still running. My breath is a bit shallow like I'm trying to suck air in through a straw but I'll be damned if I'm going to drop. I will not drop. Not now. Not when someone put a plug in me with a lucky shot after he was already dead.

I catch a flash of beige streaking through a gap in warehouses a block away and hear the bass blast of a big rig's horn followed by a screech of brakes and tires locking up as they cling to asphalt. Whatever happened slowed Carla's escape and may be my only hope because I don't have a plan anymore, certainly don't have one for Carla, and as soon as she shakes me she'll kill Risina, I know it, and I won't let that happen, can't let that happen. She might've thought better of holding a hostage and already finished the job, but fuck if I'm going to think about that . . .

I throw the taxi into a hard right to chase the sound of the semi's horn and as I whip behind the industrial plant, I just have time to see my rental car untangle itself from the left bumper of a cannery big rig.

I don't know what parts of Carla's story were bunk but I'm guessing she hasn't spent a lot of time as hunted rather than hunter, because she's panicking at the exact moment when she should have calmly made her getaway, disappeared around a corner and then I would have been lost.

The taxi has a fractured bumper and the alignment is pulling to the right but the engine is still functioning and the wheel responds to my jerks. I've spent the last few years with gunsights on me and despite the pain in my chest, despite the way my right arm is shutting down, hanging uselessly, the bullet wound worse than I thought, goddamn, I'm glad to be pursuing, chasing, closing, hunting. At least I have that. If I'm going to die, I'm going to die on offense.

I saw her knock Risina unconscious, and that image—that visual of this haggard woman repeatedly pounding Risina in the head with the butt of her gun—will sustain me until I catch Carla and kill her, bullet in my chest be damned.

The rental sedan blows through a red light and I don't hesitate, don't brake, just keep the accelerator pinned like I'm trying to stomp the pedal into the street. The taxi sways all over the road like a bird with a clipped wing and I hug the middle of the asphalt steadily, closing the distance with every swerve Carla makes.

She brakes into a hard right at the next intersection, swinging wide, and I'm able to cut the corner and narrow the gap between us to the length of a car. A UPS truck pulls out into our path and Carla swerves around it while I shoot the gap on the other side and when we bullet past the truck, I emerge right on her bumper.

Risina's head rises in the Taurus's passenger seat as she regains her senses.

No. *No no no no no no no.* Stay down, play dead, pretend to be out, don't call attention to yourself. Don't dangle bait in front of a desperate animal.

I wish these thoughts straight into Risina's brain, but she doesn't get the message. I see her head wobble and then her face turns towards Carla in the driver's seat. Even at eighty miles per hour, I can see this taking place through the back windshield as clearly as if I were in the front row of a stage play. Risina slowly comprehending her position. Carla quickly deciding she has a better chance of losing me if she doesn't have to deal with a living, breathing passenger. You can't keep a wild dog near by if you don't want to get bit. She raises her pistol to shoot Risina in the face at close range.

I upshift and tag her bumper just as she pulls the trigger. The gun jerks and fires, blowing out the rear passenger window. Startled into sobriety, Risina launches for Carla's face, going for her eyes with her fingernails leading the way.

I plow into the sedan's bumper again and this time our cars lock up and spin and twist and crumple and the world turns weightless before a blackness drops over me as suddenly as if a bag were thrown over my head.

The car is smoking and buckled but there are no emergency lights strobing through my eyelids, no sirens pounding my eardrums, so the collision must've just happened and though

I was out momentarily, it must not have been for long. The taxi is upright, still centered on all four tires though it must've flipped at least once. The pain in my chest is pure heat, like someone is holding an iron to the spot, and I can't so much as raise my elbow or curl the fingers of my right hand. Whatever damage the bullet caused was exacerbated by the wreck, and patches of light swim in and out of my vision like a swarm of gnats.

*Out. I have to climb out of the car.*

My door won't budge, but the window is gone. Half the breakaway glass is in my hair, on my face, in my lap. With my good arm, I hoist myself through the opening while I bite my lip to keep from losing consciousness. Somehow, I pull myself into a sitting position, half in and half out of the car, then look around and spot the rental sedan on its back, tires up, rocking on its spine like a dog submissively showing its belly, overpowered.

Risina emerges from the passenger window and simultaneously, Carla crawls out of the driver's side, all elbows and knees, a clutch of metal in her right hand. She's managed to hold on to her pistol.

They both rise to their feet at the same time, body and shadow, mirror images, only the inverted wreck between them to throw off the symmetry.

Carla raises her pistol, a look of disbelief, of exasperation, of disgust on her face, and I spill out of the taxi, stumble, find my feet, no weapon, no gun, nothing, just an impossible gap, a gulf, the beginning and end of life between us. I charge Carla like a demon, and I don't hear my voice but I know I'm screaming, and I don't hear my footsteps but I know I'm running as fast as I've ever run, and the gun still points at Risina who stands like an offering waiting for the sacrifice, resigned to die fifteen feet from the barrel.

"Carla!" I shout as loud as a cannon, but I know I'll never reach her in time.

As though I willed it to be, the mutt-faced woman swings the revolver toward me and Risina anticipates the distraction and closes on her like a pouncing cat and the gun goes off, but the bullet ricochets off the pavement near my feet before it spins off to God knows where.

Risina tackles Carla to the ground and drives her elbow into the woman's jaw while her other hand wrenches the gun from her grasp.

I have thirty more feet to go before I can help. From my periphery, I see vans race up from various directions, insects swarming an open wound, black vans, unmarked, at least four of them but how can I be sure? I feel like I'm moving underwater now, swimming, hallucinating.

Twenty more feet and Risina straddles Carla and drives her elbow like a piston again and again into Carla's nose. Wham, wham, wham.

The vans blow past me and screech to a halt in the intersection.

Ten more feet and Risina levels Carla's gun. Men spill out of the van just as I arrive, suited men, dark men, and Risina points the weapon directly into Carla's face and pulls the trigger.

The concussive sound of the gunshot is like a bomb going off as two men sweep me off my feet in a dead run and my head hits the ground and the world snuffs out as dark as death.

# CHAPTER THIRTEEN

**W**ould you listen to a story told by a dying man? You've been with me this long. I owe you. I owe . . .

The bullet is out of my chest, and clean dressing and a suture are packed over the wound, but the right side of my body is numb. An oxygen mask covers my nose and mouth, but I still can't seem to suck in enough air. A light shines in my face, but I can't see past the bulb and whatever that damn machine is that pings with each heartbeat is pinging slowly, irregularly, a submarine's sonar that can't seem to locate an enemy.

It takes all my energy to twist my head to the side. I'm not in a hospital, that much is clear. This is a makeshift medical room that looks like it was cobbled together in a dilapidated warehouse. Piles of what appear to be sewing machines are stacked in a corner next to discarded reams of fabric. A few folding tables line the far wall. A leg is twisted on one and it leans over like a disabled man missing a crutch. Sewing machines seem fitting for some reason I can't quite put together. My thoughts are jumbled, like I'm trying to read the contents of a folded letter through an envelope held up to the light.

The bed I'm lying atop isn't a bed, just another folding table with a mattress stuck on it. The IV I'm hooked up to and the pinging machine look authentic but what do I know? I haven't spent much time in hospitals.

Risina. Did I see her shoot Carla in the face at close range? Did I pass out before that? Something keeps shaking my brain. She wrenched Carla's gun away, jammed it in the woman's face, pulled the trigger and then I was pitching sideways like a sailboat tossed in high winds and then ping, ping, ping, here in this warehouse doubling as a clinic and I can't catch my breath and Risina, ping, Risina, ping, Risina . . .

Footsteps approach and I don't have the energy to feign unconsciousness. I feel a thumb press my eyelids open and then a penlight shines into my eyes as a man with a tight beard frowns in my face. If I weren't so drained, if I could even lift my right hand from my side, I might try to wrestle that penlight from his hand and bury it into the side of his neck until his throat lit up like a fucking runway, but I can't seem to muster the strength.

"Can you talk?" he asks after he checks my pulse.

I shake my head, or at least I think I shake my head, and his frown grows more pronounced.

He turns to another man standing over his shoulder, a man I didn't realize was in the room. "It's not good."

"Chances?"

"Fifty-fifty."

The other man bullies past the first and lowers himself inches from my nose. After a moment's inspection, he says, "I'd take that bet," then spins and exits my field of vision, if not the room.

I've never seen either man in my life.

I tried to change but I couldn't. Ping. I thought I'd evolved but I hadn't. Ping. I thought I could protect her but I couldn't. Ping. I thought I could end this but I didn't. Ping.

With each ping, my pulse seems louder, steadier. I can feel it in my throat, the ends of my fingers, my earlobes. I've never defaulted on a job, not one, and the only times I've failed to make a kill were by my own volition. This isn't a job, but the path was the same. Someone put my name on paper and I killed him for it. Someone else hired him to do it, "dark men" he called them, and I'm going to kill them all. Every last one of them. If they hurt Risina, if they touched her, they're all going to die.

My fingertips. Ping.

I can feel the pulse there, yes, and now that I concentrate, I can flex the fingers. They don't do more than twitch, but they *do* twitch. It's not much but it's something. Maybe Spilatro's bullet didn't cause as much damage as I presumed, maybe I'm not paralyzed, maybe I'm not going to die.

*I owe. I owe . . .*

I know that focusing on a goal can increase your chances at recovery, that pledging to see one last relative, one last birthday, one last wedding, one last reunion can help the dying live for days, weeks, months longer than a doctor or surgeon thought possible.

Whatever they did to her, are doing to her, that's what I have to use to sustain me, to heal me. Hatred I can let grow inside me to replace the pain. Ping. Hatred I can let flow inside me as warm as medicine. Ping. I'm going to kill these motherfuckers, these dark men, and I'm not going to die before I get the chance to bury them.

I owe . . . I owe . . .

Can I bend my elbow? I concentrate solely on my right arm as I will it to flex. It responds, only a millimeter of movement, probably invisible to anyone but me. But it was there; I felt it. Ping.

A woman enters and breathes onions into my face while she checks my pulse, my blood pressure. I crack my eyes just enough to see that her face matches her breath.

"Back to the land of the living."

I try to respond to that unimaginative opening but my throat feels like it is filled with sand.

She holds a cup of water to my lips and I start to gag, but when she withdraws the cup I manage to croak out "more."

She returns the water and it goes down better this time, like a sudden squall washing the dust from a dry creek bed.

"Your vitals are all solidly in the green," she says. "You look rough but you're gonna live for a bit."

I cast my eyes about the room. We're alone but there are a couple of cameras affixed to the ceiling. The dark men may not be here, but they're watching.

I have to watch too. Wait and watch for a mistake. *I owe. I owe* . . . Ping.

It happens a week later. I can't be precisely sure of how much time passed, but it feels like a week. Nurse Onions has been in and out at regular intervals, what I'm guessing are eight-hour shifts, replaced by Orderly Tough Guy and Nurse Eyebrows. I did my best to extract some personal information out of each, but Onions is the only one who strung more than two words together. I haven't asked about Risina. I won't. If they already know I care for her, then I'll make them question how much. If they don't know, I'll make them think she was only my pawn.

My strength returns, slowly. I've been flexing my legs under the sheets and my arms, I've been swinging in small concentric circles just above the mattress. I hope it's unnoticeable to the cameras as I lie in the dark. I make barely enough movement to toggle a few pixels on their monitors or maybe they've figured out what I'm doing. A man named Mr. Cox used to lock me inside a house all day when I was a kid. While he was gone, I'd work on my strength until I was ready to confront him. I don't have the time or the freedom to do pushups, chin-ups, sit-ups like I did then. I'm just going to have to make a move with the strength I built from those little circles and flexes. They made a mistake not hand-cuffing me to the bedrail.

Onions enters carrying a steel tray of food. Some kind of protein shake, a peanut butter and jelly sandwich, a bowl of fruit. They haven't given me a single utensil, and that pen-light hasn't made another appearance, but sometimes larger objects can do the trick. Ping. They should have brought everything in on a paper plate. Ping.

As she moves to set the tray in my lap, I spring up with more agility then they've seen out of me since they dragged me here. I grab the tray with both hands and as Onions leans in to restrain me, I slam the flat steel into her face with every-thing I have. She spills backward but doesn't drop as a metallic clang reverberates around the warehouse. Her nose is broken, and her hands go there instinctively, as I spin the tray around like I'm twirling a football and smack her with the flat end a second time, this time to the back of the head. She topples forward on to the bed now, a moan rising up like a foghorn from somewhere deep inside her.

I hear footsteps rushing in my direction from the darkness and I'm going to have to move quickly now. I charge the foot-steps and just as Orderly Tough Guy steps into the light I hit him with the edge of the tray into the white of his throat and he falls to his knees, his strength sapped as he gasps for air.

Twirling the tray again, I set my feet like a baseball batter and swing for the fences, the flat of the tray catching him in the temple. He capsizes the rest of the way to the floor and I'm into the darkness, looking for an exit.

I find an open doorway in the corner and enter a narrow corridor only lit by emergency lights. I move quickly now, the tray curled up in my arm. A man in a suit swings out from a doorway fifteen feet away, a gun in his hand, and this might've been the end of my escape, but as he pulls the trigger, I realize he's firing a stun-gun, one of those devices that shoots out an electrode along a connecting wire. This ignorant bastard thinks we're playing a game of capture or be captured instead of life and death. The electrode flies forward and I swat it away with the tray like I'm backhanding a tennis ball, and then I fling the tray at his head. It frisbees through the air, making the sound of a ringing bell as it slices into his forehead and nearly rips his scalp off. He drops instantaneously, as though his bones and muscles turned to jelly after the flying tomahawk nearly decapitated him. I scoop up the tray on the way through the door from which he just emerged.

The room is something akin to a break room, complete with a couple of vending machines, a long table lined with folding chairs, and a microwave. I flip through drawers along a row of cabinets, nothing, nothing, nothing and then jackpot: metal silverware. I take a handful of knives, start to leave my tray behind, then think better of it and retrieve it before heading through another door.

A new hallway, this one with a sign above a door at the end of it that reads "exit," but might as well say "freedom." I'm tired, sore, a little dizzy if I took the time to admit it, but all of that is just vague wisps at the back of my brain as I glide through the corridor and hit the door in full stride.

It slams open and slaps the outside wall with a bang and I'm surprised to find it overcast outside, like the beginning of a summer storm. It might be dawn, it might be dusk, impossible to tell.

Two cars are parked in an otherwise empty lot, a pair of foreign sedans and it won't take me long to jump one, get the hell out of here, and figure out where the fuck I am before I make my next move.

Just as I approach the driver's door of the black one, a familiar voice shouts from the doorway, jolting me as abruptly as if that guard's stun-gun had sent a thousand volts into my body.

"Columbus! Wait!"

I can't believe the voice I hear. I don't even have to turn around to know who it is. I start to shake my head, my hand poised inches from the sedan's door handle.

"Hold up just a second, now," he calls out.

I turn, an about-face, and a wave of nausea suddenly springs up and threatens to cloud my vision. The first drops of rain prick my head, cold.

"Archie?"

It comes out more of a question than a statement, like he might disappear, a mirage.

"First thing I gotta say before you hit me with that silver tray, Columbus. I wasn't part of this. Not directly."

He doesn't disappear. The rain starts to fall harder but he's really there, wet but not washing away.

"What the hell's going on, Archie?" In my mind I say this calmly, but I can hear it come out with a sharp edge.

"Well, I can answer that. I will, too. But what say you come back inside and we talk about it out of this mess."

"What'd they do to you, Archie?"

"Come inside, Columbus."

"If you think I'm walking back inside that warehouse, you've forgotten everything you know about me."

He nods at that as the rain accumulates in his close-cropped afro. "You gonna make me talk about this in the rain, aint'cha? Goddam."

He steps away from the warehouse door and approaches as cautiously as a bird looking for breadcrumbs under an occupied park bench.

"Second thing I gotta say is I didn't know."

"What didn't you know?"

"Can we at least sit in that car to do this?"

"Only if we drive it away from here."

"Sold."

I ready my elbow to smash in the sedan's window. "Wait!"

He holds up a set of keys. "That's my rental."

"Then you drive."

"As long as you don't kill me before I tell you what for."

"Depends on what your answers are, Archie." I slide into the passenger seat and wait for the car to come to life. The rain patters the windshield like gunfire.

A back booth at Dunkin Donuts admits us a place to talk and eat, two of Archie's favorite pastimes.

"It all played out how you know it. Some men put hands on me in the middle of the night. I put up a fight and they cracked me till I was flat. I didn't know it was Spilatro or the Agency or none of that. No one told me this was coming. You gotta believe that. I meant what I said when I said I'd help you stay gone."

Archie doesn't smile as much as he used to. That was his trademark, flashing his teeth, making you feel comfortable, even when you thought maybe he was trying to pull one over on you. Maybe after his sister died, he couldn't bring himself to put on that show anymore. Or maybe this business with the government shook him up.

"How long have you been working for Uncle Sam?"

"Not working for. Working *with*. There's a continent of difference between those two prepositions."

He bites into a cinnamon twist, but doesn't look down, his eyes stoic.

"Any fence worth a whit does some Agency shit time to time. They outsource the domestic bloodshed. It's their culture. They use their talent on foreign soil, but back home? They contract out the wetwork, same as everyone. You've done a job or two for them over the years, guaranteed."

"I don't care."

He holds up his palms defensively, like he wants me to let him finish. He hasn't dropped his hands below the table since we arrived.

"I know you don't, Columbus. You a Silver Bear and you don't look to know who hired you. A kill's a kill and it's all about the hunt. I get that. I'm just trying to put some background on this thing we're in."

He coughs into his fist, like he's still sorting out his thoughts. "Some people in the government found out you was the one what killed that senator . . ."

"Congressman."

"Politician. Presidential candidate. Abe Mann. Whatever. We on the same page."

"How'd they know it was me?"

"They got a name and that's all they got. Contractor named Columbus did it. There are only a few like you in the whole damn world, so the field was narrow. Who knows how the whisper became a fact, but they knew, and when they found out it was you, they found out about me."

The cinnamon twist is gone and after he licks the sugar crystals off his fingers, he's on to an old-fashioned.

"They knew you'd given up the game, and they hired Spilatro to bring you back. He's the cat who came up with the kidnap plan, the ransom note, the bread crumb trail that would bring you out of hiding."

"So these men could have revenge on me for killing their candidate, their puppet."

Archie sets down his donut. "Not exactly."

I wait for more.

"They want you to work for them."

I shake my head, my mouth twisted in a frown. "Do I look like I have a bump on my head, Archie? Why would I buy that?"

"Because it's the truth. They saw the job you pulled in Los Angeles and wanted to know the man who could execute like that and walk away clean. They got beat by you, and dark men like them do one of two things when they get beat. They either fix the problem by plugging it up, or they recruit the son-of-a-bitch over to their side. Except with you, they figured best to do both."

I don't think my head has stopped shaking.

Archie continues, undaunted, "They went to their best hitter inside the company and said, 'here's your assignment. You find this Columbus and you kill him.' But what they were really saying was 'let the best man win.'"

"A test?"

"Something like that. *Competition's* a better word. They want to run a stable with the best horses. And you just proved again you're the best in the game."

"And you played along?"

"After the beatdown they put on me, they drove me to what they call a 'secure location.' Then the real players showed up and told me the what-all. They kept me fed, let me watch TV, but they made it clear they wasn't fucking around. Wanted to keep me alive and kicking so I could broker a deal if you bested Spilatro. And so here we are."

"And Smoke is dead."

His eyes cloud over. "Yeah. It's a fuckin' shame Spilatro did him like that. Smoke was good people."

I sit back and fold my arms. "Call 'em over here."

Archie gets that look on his face I've seen before, the one that says he forgot who he was dealing with. He wipes his fingers carefully with a napkin, then leans back and lets loose a long sigh. Finally, he cranes his neck and nods at the corner booth.

Two men wearing charcoal suits rise from the booth as they try unsuccessfully to keep their faces blank.

Archie slides around next to me, and they sit opposite.

"And the third. Call him over."

The shorter of the two men—the one with bushy, black eyebrows that seem too large for his face—calls out to a third suited man perched at the counter. "Grayson, you're made."

A man at the counter slumps his shoulders, turns around, and pulls over a chair to the end of the table. The three men look approximately the same age—late forties—and all have hard eyes that indicate they've seen a lot of shit most people reserve for nightmares.

"You're the dark men, huh?"

Bushy Eyebrows speaks up. "I'm Mitchells. This is Vancill. And Grayson's at the end there."

"You ordered all this?"

Mitchells shrugs. "I ordered your elimination. You cost us a great deal of time, effort and expense when you put our candidate in a bodybag."

"He set it up."

"But you killed him."

"And now you want me to work for you?"

He smiles. "We happen to have an opening."

"Go fuck yourself."

Mitchells sniffs the air like he just caught a whiff of something unpleasant.

"That's warranted, so I'll let it slide. But you're a very smart man, Columbus, so I won't let it slide twice. There are advantages to working for us that I know will be attractive to you. Namely, you'll get to keep doing what you love doing the most."

"I was out."

"Were you?" He says this without a smile. "I'm trained to read people the way my colleagues are trained to crack code. I've watched your progress on this mission and before it . . . all over Europe for the preceding three years. Prague, Belgium, Spain, Paris. You're a killer, you're good at killing, and I'll be damned if you don't enjoy it. I don't know any plainer way to say it."

He doesn't look like he's a man who flatters as a matter of course, and if this is an attempt at flattery, it's a clumsy one. Rather, he simply speaks the truth and says it plain. "I would've sought you out sooner, would've tried to pull you in, but you stepped off the grid after you fell for the bookstore owner in Rome. That made it difficult to find you, and it would've been irresponsible for me not to make sure you hadn't lost a step once we did."

He watches my eyes to see if his casual mention of Risina elicits a response.

"So this was all about pulling me in?"

"This was about making sure you were worth pulling in. My team here thinks you are. I think the jury's out."

He says it levelly, a challenge there. Then to emphasize the point, "You gonna ask about the girl?"

"You know her name. You can say it."

"Risina Lorenzana. You gonna ask about her or you want to keep pretending she doesn't matter?"

"You want to keep poking me until you find out the answer?" I try to match his expression, but I'm not sure I pull it off.

He settles back. The other two haven't said a word and Archie just chews on his old-fashioned donut like it's the only thing in the room.

"All right," I say after a charged moment. "Let's hear your offer."

Mitchells folds his fingers together. "It's simple. You take your assignments from us. You give us a break on your rate. You keep working through Archie if you want, but we'll supplement his fieldwork with our intel. And if you get caught or captured, you put a bullet in your own head. Otherwise, your life won't change much. You won't be lying on a beach in a fishing village, but we won't overwork you either."

"And there's no getting out?"

"You put a few years in and then we talk again. We're not inflexible."

"And what about Risina?"

If he says "what *about* her?" or cracks a smile, I'm going to leap across the table and kill him with my bare hands. But he must have told the truth when he said he was good at reading people because he adds no emotion to his voice when he says, "She's free to go. You want to keep her in play, that's your decision."

"I want her to be my fence."

Archie stops in mid-bite and looks at me out of the tops of his eyes.

"Fine," says Mitchells.

"You trying to cut me out after all we been through? Let me tell you something . . ."

"Don't get nervous. She's going to need some better training than I could give her. I know how to close a contract but I don't know shit about fence-work. I want you to show her the ropes."

That seems to mollify Archie. He jabs his index finger into the table to make the point. "I'll set her up square. I promise you that."

I nod but I'm not ready to look him in the eye. It'll have to be enough.

Mitchells unfolds his hands. "We have a deal then?"

"We have a deal."

The dark men get up from the booth, including Archie, and start to shuffle away, satisfied.

Mitchells takes a step toward the door, then turns around and puts his hands on the table.

"And Columbus?"

"Yeah."

"I also know your name," he says.

# EPILOGUE

I drive to a country house in rural Virginia, about twenty miles outside of Charlottesville. Mitchells gave me an address where Risina would be safe, and if he's lying, I'm hard pressed to figure out his play. They could've killed me in the aftermath of the Spilatro climax instead of freeing a bullet from my chest and sewing me up, instead of making me whole. They don't want me angry; there's no benefit to it. Right?

Farms with red barns, with tin silos, with white-post fences, with black cattle, with green grass in wide pastures pass outside my windshield like Ansel Adams photographs of a forgotten America. The sun hangs on the horizon and burns the clouds above it a malevolent red. The contrast between the farms and the sky is disquieting, as though doom hangs over placidity like a guillotine waiting to drop.

She is a tiger. She said it and she did the job and when the time came to pull the trigger, she fired the gun into a woman's face at point-blank range. She didn't shy away from the mess when it interfered with our life and everything she's done since Smoke showed up has been smart and efficient.

This could work. This could be better than how I imagined it. She'll have Archie to guide her and the intel of the Agency to supplement her, and I can't discount her innate passion and quick mind. She could be a great fence, the best I've had since Pooley. She'll surpass Archie in short order, I'm sure of it. I won't just be a horse in a stable to her, I'll be her only horse, and she'll do whatever it takes to ensure my success, the way Pooley used to perform the job when I first started. It can work. It will work.

Did the bloodshed change her? Did the battle sour her stomach? Will she want to disappear again, now that she's seen up close what a pistol can do to a human face? Will she want to run? Will she want to flee alone?

The road turns to gravel as the GPS tells me I have less than a mile to go. I'm nervous in a way I haven't been for a long time. We've been driving forward since this started, no time to catch our breath, no time to reflect, and now that she's had some moments apart, will she pull out of the spiral? Will she emerge like a repatriated prisoner, free from Stockholm Syndrome, with a fresh realization that this life was an illusion, a fantasy, and the reality is so much worse?

No. It can't be that way. I know her. Everything we've shared since I walked into that bookstore in Rome has been real, permanent, fervid. We were already solid, but now that we've been through the trenches together, we're unbreakable.

She can be a great fence. She proposed it and she meant it. She said I have to be all the way in with her and I am. I swear I am. We can do this together.

I reach a red mailbox with the address number stenciled in black on its side and turn the car through a gate, bump over a cattle guard, and head down a bumpy road through a forest. She proposed it. She knows my fearful symmetry. She always knew it.

The road clears and on a hill sits a simple white house.

She must hear me coming because she's through the front door, blinking away tears as soon as I'm out of the driver's side. We meet halfway up the sidewalk and are in each other's arms and it's as it was, as it will be. This can work. We can make it work. She can be my fence, and I'll be her assassin and we'll make it work.

She pulls back, her face wet, her eyes shiny.

"I'm pregnant," she says.

CPSIA information can be obtained
at www.ICGtesting.com
Printed in the USA
LVHW021544040419
612997LV00016B/753